Kendra's anger exploded . . .

Kendra couldn't stand another minute of Ariane's taking her things. It had to stop!

Suddenly, there was a loud cracking noise at the window. Veins of light fractured the panes of glass. Then, with a sudden violent explosion, the window burst apart. A storm of broken glass flew out into the room. One large, jagged piece sliced through the air, shining like a knife blade as it flew straight toward Ariane and Graham!

THE THRILL

MIDNIGHT Secrets

Volume II THE THRILL

WOLFF RYP

WESTWIND®
Troll Associates

Printed in the United States of America.

10 9 8 7 6 5 4 3 2 1

PROLOGUE

Kendra sleeps peacefully under the silken covers of her bed. For many months, no nightmares have troubled her rest. She no longer fears the midnight visitor—the golden man who awakened her with his horrible demands and inhuman passion. She no longer suffers from the agony of longing for him. The thrill she once felt in his dizzying embrace has faded. He spoke of love, but he brought terror. Now the horror that once invaded her life is gone. She defeated the monster that threatened her and all those she loved. She alone destroyed her enemy and freed them all.

Now that he is gone, Kendra's memories have faded. She no long remembers the months of terror. She can sleep easily, in calm forgetfulness, without fear.

◆ ◆ ◆

Kendra breathes deeply and turns her head on her pillow. She doesn't hear the faint bell-song of crystal chimes. She doesn't see the swirling lights beginning to gather in the corner of her dark room.

Like a cloud of fireflies, the lights dance closer to the bed. They bend over Kendra, almost as if they are kissing her. Suddenly, the lights change shape. A man appears in their place, shining in the dark. He is handsome, with golden hair and piercing blue eyes. He stands at the side of her bed, his face glowing with pleasure as he studies the sleeping girl. He whispers, "You are so beautiful," just as he has done so often before.

Revell.

He bends closer and says softly, "Kendra, I've been waiting so eagerly for you. I've come for you now."

He smiles tenderly and shakes his head. "You thought you had destroyed me. But I need your power. We are meant to be together—always." For a long time, he watches her sleeping peacefully. Then, gently, he lifts her limp hand and kisses it. She doesn't wake.

Slowly, the dancing lights surround him. The music of the chimes fade. The lights fracture and vanish.

He is gone. But his quiet voice lingers in the room as the darkness closes in again: "I am your destiny!"

CHAPTER 1

Kendra Linton stretched, then climbed out of bed. The bright sun was streaming in the window through the lacy curtains. It was another beautiful summer day.

How lucky, she thought dreamily. Her boyfriend, Neil Jarmon, was coming over later to play tennis, and the weather had once again cooperated with their plans.

Suddenly, the rose-colored birthmark on the back of Kendra's hand began to tingle.

That's weird, she thought. Ever since she was a little girl, the birthmark had tingled like this—especially right before something unexpected or dangerous was about to happen. It had been a long time since she'd felt the prickle.

Maybe my hand fell asleep, Kendra told herself, determined to dismiss the unexpected warning. She shook her hand, trying to get the blood flowing. The day was too beautiful to spend it worrying about something that might—or might not—happen.

She grabbed her bathrobe, then went to take a quick shower.

A few minutes later, Kendra stood in front of the window, toweling her long dark hair dry. The noise of construction out on the street pounded in her ears. Skeleton-like fingers of steel beams jabbed at the bright blue of the late summer sky. In front of the mansion where Kendra lived on 76th Street in New York City, a high-rise apartment building was being constructed. When it was completed, the building would hide her house from the view of people walking by on the street. Kendra didn't mind one bit. At last she and her family would get some privacy. Now people on the street were always stopping to gawk at the old mansion behind the heavy iron gates.

Kendra would never forget how she had come to live in the mansion. One afternoon, her mother, Dinah, had introduced Kendra and her sister, Lauren, to Graham Vanderman and told them she had just married him. Then, as if that weren't enough of a shock, Dinah had announced they'd all be moving from their Fifth Avenue apartment to Graham's massive house on 76th Street.

When Kendra caught her first glimpse of the house, she couldn't ever imagine living there. It looked like something from a horror movie. It had tall, looming spires and an old family cemetery on the grounds.

Now, many months later, Kendra had come to

love the old house with its high ceilings, rambling rooms, and beautiful gardens and lawns.

Sometimes, however, Kendra had the vague sense that she wasn't safe here. That something had happened to her in this house. Something thrilling—but horrifying. If only she could remember what it was.

She turned from the sunny window and shook out her damp wavy hair. Slipping into white tennis shorts and a T-shirt, she crossed the hall to her sister's room.

Lauren was curled up in bed, breathing deeply. A lock of her long blonde hair was twirled around one finger. The crashing of the construction work outside didn't wake her—she could even sleep through the loudest rock music.

Kendra smiled at the sight of her fifteen-year-old sister. Asleep, Lauren looked as innocent as a baby. Kendra had always felt protective of her younger sister, especially after their father had died nearly nine years ago. Dinah was too distracted to pay much attention to them, so the girls turned to each other for support. There wasn't anything Kendra wouldn't do for Lauren.

Except let her sleep away a gorgeous summer day.

"Tennis?" Kendra said cheerfully. "Swimming? A chance to ride Vinnie in the Kentucky Derby?"

Lauren stirred. Vinnie was her beloved Arabian stallion, and the mere mention of his name was enough to wake her.

"Come on. Get up. At least take Vinnie for a trot in the park. He's getting fat and lazy, and none of the other horses will talk to him."

"Go away, whoever you are," Lauren groaned and burrowed deeper under the covers.

"I'm your conscience. You're wasting a beautiful day. And summer's nearly over."

"Pest," Lauren mumbled.

"Okay, my final offer. If you get up now, I'll let you wear my red beaded mini next time we go to a club. The one with the silver fringe."

"And the sandals, too?" Lauren murmured sleepily.

"Right, sandals, too."

Lauren sat up groggily and squinted at Kendra. "You mean it?"

"Nope. I lied. But now that you're up . . . ."

"Hey, that was mean," Lauren declared.

"I know," Kendra replied with a grin. "But I need you to be my doubles partner. Neil is coming over later to play tennis. Call up one of your friends so we'll have a fourth."

"Okay," Lauren agreed cheerfully. She jumped out of bed and dashed toward her bathroom. "Meet you downstairs in twenty minutes."

✦ ✦ ✦

"There you are, girls. I want to talk to you."

Dinah walked into the breakfast room, looking as glamorous as a character from an old movie. She wore a filmy gray dress and, as usual, her blonde hair was perfectly styled. She poured coffee from the silver pot on the sideboard into a delicate china cup.

"I'm glad to find you two together," Dinah said, sitting across the table from Kendra and Lauren. "I have something incredible to tell you." She put her cup down after a sip and leaned toward her daughters.

"Now, what do you think of this? I've decided to send you both to school in Switzerland at the start of the new semester. Isn't that exciting! It's a marvelous school—of course, very difficult to get into, but with Graham's connections you've both already been accepted."

Kendra stared at her mother, not believing what she was hearing.

"Now, don't look so surprised, Kendra," Dinah went on. "It isn't as if we never talked about your having a year abroad. And you'll be going to one of the very best girls' boarding schools in the world—very advanced. How lucky you are! I wish I'd had such an opportunity when I was your age. Imagine, skiing the Alps—the best teachers . . . ."

As her mother rambled on, Kendra tried to contain her anger. How could Dinah spring another change on them like this? Kendra had always hoped to spend a year abroad—but she wanted to talk about it first. Not just have her mother make all the arrangements without even consulting her.

She looked at Lauren to see how she was taking the news. Her sister looked as surprised as Kendra felt.

"Can I bring Vinnie?" Lauren asked.

"Certainly not, but they have horses there—and absolutely everything else—and I'll arrange for you to ride, and we'll make sure that Vinnie is well cared for while you're away."

"I think he'll go nuts without me," Lauren said.

Kendra frowned, remembering the time Vinnie went wild in Central Park and tried to trample Lauren. It had never happened before—and it hadn't happened since. But the fact that her sister had nearly been killed still bothered Kendra.

"Never mind Vinnie," Dinah said impatiently. "Any girl your age would be thrilled at the chance for such an adventure. A year in Switzerland at such a wonderful school. Oh, I know you're going to love it!"

As Lauren began asking questions about the school's stable and the curriculum, Kendra could see her sister was beginning to get excited.

"Will we be living in a huge dormitory, with lots of foreign girls?" Lauren asked.

"Heavens, no!" Dinah exclaimed. "All the girls have their own rooms. I told you, it's a very elegant school—very famous. The students come from all over the world—why, kings and presidents and movie stars all send their daughters there. You'll meet so many interesting people."

"Great," Kendra muttered. All she could think of was how hard it would be to leave Neil—and the television workshop at her school, Wilbraham Academy. Kendra had recently decided she wanted to become a TV news anchorperson, and the studio workshop at Wilbraham was excellent preparation. "But what about my TV workshop?" Kendra asked.

"You'll have plenty of time for that in college," Dinah said. "This is a great opportunity, Kendra, and you should be thrilled at the chance to see more of the world. I know I would have been!"

"Do I have a choice?" Kendra said between clenched teeth. "It sounds like you've already arranged everything."

"I certainly have," Dinah said with obvious pride. "And it wasn't easy, either. Convincing your headmaster at Wilbraham that it was in your best interests took all my powers of persuasion, I can tell you. Sometimes I wonder if that man has any spirit of adventure."

"I think it sounds great, Kennie," Lauren coaxed her. "I love adventures, don't you? And we'll be together, anyhow, so it'll be just like home."

"Not exactly," Kendra told her sister. She turned to Dinah. "When do we leave?"

"In a couple of weeks." Dinah beamed. "Summer's almost over, so we can spend the time shopping and getting you ready and making sure that—Lauren! Don't put so much butter on your toast. Think of your figure, please!"

Kendra almost snorted with annoyance. Lauren was as slender as Kendra. Neither one of them had to worry about her weight. But it was Dinah's latest notion that they should all look as starved as the waif-like models in her fashion magazines.

Kendra crumpled up her napkin and tossed it on the table. Dinah was still chattering to Lauren about the clothes she'd need for Switzerland when Kendra stood up and slipped out the front door.

Neil was just coming up the front path, tennis racket under his arm.

She rushed toward him, and the news about going to school in Switzerland tumbled out even before she said hello.

✦ ✦ ✦

The night air was cool, now that summer was almost over. Kendra had thrown a denim jacket around her shoulders when she and Neil decided to walk around the grounds of the house after dinner.

"Why don't you tell her no—just say that you don't want to go?" Neil asked for the hundredth time. They had spent the whole day together, feeling miserable and trying to figure out how to convince Dinah to let Kendra stay at home.

She held his hand as they walked along the cliff on the high pathway overlooking the East River. Through the trees lining the path, she could see the lights of bridges and buildings twinkling across the water. Down at the bottom of the sheer drop of the cliff, the lights made wobbly reflections in the rippling water. Under different circumstances, the view would have been romantic. But today they were both too depressed to enjoy it.

"What's up, Kendra? You can usually get your own way with Dinah." Neil continued to press her.

Kendra sighed. "I know, but she seems so determined. She's got everything arranged already, and Lauren seems so excited."

"Maybe Lauren should go by herself. She's old enough to be on her own, and it wouldn't be so bad for her to get away from you for a while."

"Thanks a lot!" Kendra shot back. "I don't want her to have to go alone."

"What about me?" Neil teased her gently. "I'll be alone, too—it'll be horrible. Don't you care?"

She stopped and turned to him. "Of course I do."

Neil smiled and slipped his arms around her. He bent close. She turned her face up to meet his. His kiss was warm and sweet. As they held each other tightly, Kendra felt a terrible sadness. She was truly miserable at the thought of leaving him.

Suddenly, a beautiful sound wafted on the air. It was a soft tinkling song, the music of crystal chimes swaying in a gentle breeze. To Kendra it sounded like music from a dream—strangely familiar, but she couldn't place it. The sound was beautiful, yet haunting. Kendra had the oddest feeling that it was calling to her.

She pulled away from Neil abruptly, trying to listen. But the music was gone.

"What is it?" Neil asked. "You're thinking. Are you going to change your mind?"

"I—I can't. Please don't ask me again. You're making me feel worse."

She spun around and stepped out of reach of his arms. Her hair caught on a low-hanging branch.

"Ow!" she cried. Kendra struggled to free herself, but her hair had tangled badly on the branch.

"Here, let me."

Neil stepped to the edge of the cliff and reached out. Without warning, the ground under his feet crumbled. He pitched forward over the edge of the cliff and began to topple down the slope. Tumbling over and over, he plunged down the rocky slide, down toward the water below.

Kendra's eyes opened wide with horror. "Neil!" Her screams filled the air. "Neil!"

While she stood helplessly watching, Neil was falling to his death.

CHAPTER 2

Kendra's shrill cries pierced the night air.

Neil's body rolled faster and faster down the cliff.

This can't be happening, she thought desperately.

A strange word flashed into her head: "Patience." What could it mean? In her mind, she saw another body rolling down the cliff—the body of a young girl. Suddenly, Kendra knew the girl's name: "Patience Anne Tudor." She was someone from long, long ago who had plunged down the cliff at that very same spot—and drowned in the river below. Her body lay in the family cemetery. But how did I know how she died?

Frantically, no longer thinking, Kendra pulled her tangled hair from the branch and shouted, "No! Don't!"

A loud grunt rose from halfway down the slope. Then the night was suddenly silent.

Trembling fearfully, Kendra peered over the lip of the cliff.

Neil's body was wrapped around the stump of a tree trunk.

His deadly fall had been stopped. But he wasn't moving.

"Neil?" Kendra called.

He didn't answer.

"Neil?" Her voice cracked as she stared down at him. Tears stung Kendra's eyes. She began to shudder. "Oh, Neil!" she sobbed in anguish.

Suddenly, a moan rose from Neil's body. His arms began to twitch. His head turned.

He's alive! Kendra breathed a sigh of relief. She scrambled down the cliff until she reached him. "Are you okay?"

Neil was breathing heavily as he lay flat on his back. "I think so," he said slowly. He raised himself to a sitting position, wincing. When he looked at Kendra, his eyes were wide with fear. "I couldn't stop myself. I slipped . . . ."

"I know. I know." She leaned down and reached a hand out to him. "Come on. Let's get you back to the house. Can you walk?"

He nodded. "I'm okay. I just feel like a jerk. One minute I was on solid ground, and the next, I was tumbling down that cliff. I don't know what happened. It was as if—well, the ground crumbled under me."

Kendra bit her lip, puzzled. How could the ground just give way like that?

She helped him up, and they slowly made their

way back to the house. Neil leaned heavily on Kendra, limping and groaning occasionally as they climbed the front steps.

Inside they told Dinah and Graham what had happened.

"You'd better get to the emergency room," Graham said.

Neil shook his head. "I'm okay, really."

But Graham insisted, and finally Neil agreed. Dinah called for a limousine for the short trip to the hospital and then called Neil's parents. While they waited, Lauren hovered worriedly over Neil, offering him everything from Pepsi to pizza. Some of the color had returned to his face, but Kendra could see he was still in pain.

At last, the limousine arrived. Kendra and Graham helped Neil inside and rode with him to the hospital.

A few anxiety-filled hours later, they were all relieved to learn that Neil hadn't broken anything. He had plenty of bruises, and a small gash on his forehead needed three stitches, but that was the worst of it. The doctor let him go home with his parents.

By the time Graham and Kendra returned to the house, it was after midnight.

Graham squeezed Kendra's shoulder. "Why don't you get some sleep? It's been a long night."

"It sure has," she agreed. "'Night, Graham. Thanks for getting Neil to the hospital." She smiled gratefully at him.

"See you in the morning," he said, returning her smile.

Kendra climbed the stairs to her room, thinking about Graham. When Dinah had first announced her marriage to him, Kendra hadn't exactly been thrilled. A few months' warning would have been nice. But ever since Kendra and Lauren had moved into Graham's house, he and his son, Anthony, had been wonderful to them. Last spring, Graham had even built the pool and tennis court so the girls could have friends over this summer.

Still, there was something vaguely mysterious about Graham. All she really knew about her stepfather was that he had been married twice before, and both wives had died at a young age. Both in tragic circumstances.

Kendra paused in thought on the stairs. There was something else about Graham, wasn't there? Something she had once overheard him say when he didn't know she was listening. He had been talking to—someone terrifying. Who? She hadn't seen Graham or the man he was talking to. But Graham's words echoed suddenly in her head: "You've done enough damage. You must not cause any more pain."

She shook her head. Had that really happened? She wasn't even sure. She couldn't remember anything else. She continued up the stairs to her room.

Lauren was lying on Kendra's bed, waiting nervously for news about Neil. Lying beside her on the floor was Max, Graham's big black Labrador retriever, who followed Lauren wherever she went.

Lauren sat up as Kendra entered the room. "Is Neil okay, Kennie?"

"Yes," Kendra reported happily. She told Lauren about Neil's injuries, which were amazingly minor. "I can't believe he wasn't hurt worse. I saw him fall down that cliff. He could have been killed." She shook her head. "You know, I still don't understand how it happened. Neil's a super athlete. He's not someone who loses his balance."

"Yeah, you're right. But the important thing is that he's okay." Lauren yawned and stood up. "I'm beat. I guess I'll go to bed now. 'Night, Kennie."

Max wagged his tail and padded along after her.

Kendra said goodnight, then practically stumbled into the bathroom to wash up for bed. She was exhausted by the time she crept under the covers and turned out the light.

But, tired as she was, sleep did not come right away. Instead she gazed up at the ceiling, watching shadows flicker around her room.

Kendra couldn't stop thinking about tonight's near-fatal events. What had caused Neil's fall? She couldn't believe it was just a simple accident. It was almost as if some mysterious force had attacked Neil.

That's crazy, Kendra, she told herself. His foot

slipped and he fell. Right?

But deep inside she knew that it wasn't a crazy thought. Something weird had happened today, and it was a miracle that Neil was still alive.

As she stared up at the ceiling, the birthmark on her hand began to tingle again. Danger. This time Kendra couldn't dismiss the warning as quickly as she had this morning. She had ignored the signal—and it had almost cost Neil his life.

The minutes on her digital clock ticked by. She lay awake in the darkness, gently rubbing her hand and hoping desperately that the fear which had settled deep in her bones would go away soon.

✦ ✦ ✦

Hours later, a gust of night wind blew through the open window, making the curtains billow.

The faint tinkling of crystal chimes rose on the breeze. Its delicate, airy song filled the room.

Kendra woke, startled. She listened intently. She felt confused and disoriented. Wasn't that the ghostly music she had heard on the cliff? Just before Neil had plunged over the edge?

She sat up in bed. Something was sparkling in the darkest corner of her room. It looked like a vibrating mass of tiny lights, like a cloud of fireflies. She rubbed her eyes. Fear clutched at Kendra's insides as the lights danced closer to her bed, whirling into human shape. A golden glow burst from the cloud as a young man appeared— the most handsome man she had ever seen.

Kendra drew in her breath. At first glance, the man seemed to be only a few years older than Kendra. But a closer look told her that something was different about him. He was almost ageless. He drifted over to the side of her bed. He was bathed in golden light. In the darkness, his eyes glowed and seemed to give off sparks. His blond hair tumbled around his face.

Gently he reached out and stroked Kendra's hair. She closed her eyes. His touch was light and gentle. Warmth spread through her whole body. All her worries and confusion about Neil drifted out of her head.

She rested her cheek on the man's hand, willing him to stay with her.

Who is he? Kendra thought. He was so attractive, so unlike anyone Kendra had ever seen before. Yet he seemed so familiar—as if she'd known him all her life.

"Kendra," he whispered softly. He traced the features on her face with his finger and then pressed his lips to the rosy mark on the back of her hand. His lips were like velvet. "Do you remember me?"

She shook her head. Somehow she couldn't find words. It was as if she were dreaming or in a trance.

"I have been waiting for you through all the centuries," he said. "I am yours and you are mine."

He dropped her hand, and Kendra almost winced in pain. She longed for him to touch her again, to hold her in his arms.

"Think," he prodded gently. "We've met before."

She sat up, trying to clear her head. But all she could think about was getting close to this man again. Then a vague memory of golden lights drifted into her head. A memory of this man entering her room in the past. The familiar, overwhelming longing for him. A sudden, bone-chilling terror.

"Revell."

The name burst from Kendra's lips as she shivered with fear. She backed away into her pillows.

"You remember me now," he said, smiling. He reached for her hand.

Kendra hesitated. Hazy memories flooded back into her head. She felt a burning desire for him, yet something nagged at her mind. Revell had left her, she had driven him away forever. But why?

"You thought you had destroyed me, Kendra, didn't you?" he murmured. "You have great powers. But they're still no match for mine. Not yet."

Powers? What powers? How could I have destroyed him? What is he talking about?

Kendra's mind felt foggy. Fear made her heart race. Why had Revell come back and what did he want?

"Go away. Leave me, please," Kendra pleaded. She closed her eyes, afraid to look at him. The attraction she felt for him was so strong, it frightened her.

"Don't you want to feel my arms around you again, Kendra? Yes, you do. Open your eyes, my love. Look at me."

His voice washed over her. So sweet, so compelling . . . .

She heard him slip away from her side. When he spoke again, his voice came from across the room.

"Come to me, Kendra. You want to. I know you do. And I am here, longing for you. Come into my arms, my beautiful Kendra."

Somehow she had risen from her bed as he spoke. She swayed unsteadily in the darkness. Then, in some way she couldn't understand, she felt herself floating toward him, into his arms.

When Revell bent over her and kissed her, it was more thrilling than any kiss she had ever experienced. Kendra felt her heart pound and her breathing grow shallow. It was as if she had melted into him and become part of him. She didn't ever want the kiss to end.

Finally, Revell leaned away from her to study her face. He gazed deeply, lovingly, into her eyes. At that moment, Kendra knew she would do anything he asked.

"Don't leave me, Kendra," he said. "You must stay here, in this house. We will be together always, as we were meant to be."

"Yes," she said breathlessly.

"You will not go to Switzerland."

"No."

"You will never leave me."

"No, never."

A faint smile traced the curve of Revell's lips. He sighed deeply with satisfaction. Then he stepped back. Fireflies of light began to drift across his face. His body faded into a smoky cloud.

After he had vanished, Kendra returned to her bed. Why had she been frightened? Revell wasn't dangerous. He loved her and wanted to be with her.

Hazy memories of him were dancing around inside her head. She wished she could think clearly and sort them out. Something had happened between them before—something strange. Strange, but wonderful, she reminded herself.

Kendra closed her eyes and tried to sleep. But she was on fire with excitement and longing. She wanted to feel the thrill of Revell's arms around her again. She could still taste his soft lips on hers. She thought she would faint from her desire to hold him and kiss him once more. How could she be afraid of Revell when all of her cried out for his love? Whatever had happened between them before, it was a secret that remained hidden.

But somehow it didn't matter now—the only thing Kendra cared about was finding a way to see Revell again.

CHAPTER 3

Kendra knocked gently on Dinah's bedroom door.

"May I come in?"

"Mmmm, what is it?" Dinah called sleepily. She wasn't an early riser. She was a grouchy riser. And the earlier she woke, the grouchier she was. But Kendra knew that this was the best time to catch Dinah off guard and get her to agree to whatever Kendra wanted.

She pushed open the door and entered the large darkened room.

Dinah was lolling against a mound of silky pillows in a huge bed. Piles of ivory sheets and covers buried her up to her shoulders.

Kendra tiptoed to the side of the bed.

"Couldn't it wait?" Dinah grumbled. "What time is it? Goodness, Kendra, what are you doing up so early? After all the excitement last night, I would have expected you to sleep till noon. Have you had breakfast?"

"Yes, with Graham, before he left."

"Come here, then." She sat higher against the pillows and patted the side of the bed. "Let me look at you. Your eyes are all bleary, and you look positively haggard. Don't you realize how important a good night's sleep is?"

"Yes, but I—"

"Well, what is it? What's so important that you had to get me up this early?"

"I've decided I don't want to go to Switzerland. Before you start telling me why I have to go please let me finish. There are a lot of reasons for me to stay in New York this year. I love my television course, and Mr. Taylor said he was going to put me on camera a lot more this year. He thinks I have a real chance to be a news anchor. And then there's Neil. We're just getting our relationship back on track, and I don't want to jeopardize it. I can't go."

Kendra paused and held her breath. She hoped Dinah believed the part about Neil. If she were telling her mother the truth, Kendra would have said that there was a mysterious man with haunting eyes and an indescribably sweet kiss that she could never bear to be away from.

"Really, Kendra! What's gotten into you?" Dinah raised herself up against the pillows, sighing with annoyance. "After all the trouble I went to, getting you into the best school in Europe. Do you have any idea of all the arrangements I had to make? And what about your sister? What is

Lauren supposed to do—miss the opportunity of a lifetime just because you don't feel like leaving your boyfriend?"

"Lauren's old enough to go herself," Kendra insisted. "You told us that girls go to the school from all over the world, some lots younger than Lauren, I'll bet. It'll be good for her to get away, on her own. I just can't leave. Not now."

Kendra's strategy paid off. It was too early in the morning for Dinah to put up much of a fight.

"Very well," Dinah said with a frown. "You can stay, if it means so much to you. I'll explain it to Lauren later, though I can't imagine how she'll feel about being on her own."

"I'll tell her myself," Kendra said. "I'm sure she'll understand."

Kendra really wasn't sure at all about Lauren's reaction. How could Kendra explain her reasons? Thinking of Revell, Kendra wondered how she could ever expect her sister to understand something she didn't understand herself.

Kendra shivered with excitement as she remembered Revell's kiss and the way he had wrapped his arms possessively around her. She felt her heart skip a beat. Although Kendra wasn't sure what Revell wanted from her, she was sure of one thing: she couldn't wait to see him again.

✦ ✦ ✦

"So, how's Lauren taking it?" Hallie asked as she and Kendra rested in lounge chairs at the side of the pool. They had just spent a half hour racing laps, and Kendra had won each time.

Hallie Benedict was Kendra's best friend. They were in the same grade at Wilbraham and had lived in the same apartment building on Fifth Avenue before Dinah married Graham. There wasn't a day that they didn't see each other or at least talk on the phone. Kendra was glad that Hallie had recovered from her fear of the house on 76th Street. Ever since that awful day when Hallie had gotten lost in the dark underground tunnels that honeycombed the main floor and cellar of the house, she had hated to visit. It had been a terrifying experience. Kendra didn't want to think about the horror of that day. She was just happy that Hallie felt more comfortable at the house now.

As I do, Kendra thought.

She remembered her own fear of the house when she first moved in. She would have given anything then to move back to their old, cozy apartment on Fifth Avenue with her friend Hallie only one floor below. Kendra's first sight of Graham's house had filled her with such dread that it took her breath away. But, little by little, the house had claimed her. Something about it, some spirit that pervaded every corner of the house and its grounds, had wrapped itself around her and taken possession of her. Now she knew that the spirit of the house was part of her. And it was almost as if she had always belonged there.

"Hey, Ken! Where'd you disappear to all of a sudden?" Hallie said. "I just asked if Lauren's going to chicken out about Switzerland too. Like you."

Kendra shook herself awake from remembering and reached for a dry towel. "Oh, Lauren? No, she's really excited. And I didn't chicken out, for your information. Actually, Lauren can't wait to go. It's the first time she'll be on her own. She's had a different farewell party with a different friend almost every day since she found out."

"I don't blame her," Hallie said. "Frankly, I think you've lost it. How could you pass up a chance like that? A year in Switzerland! I mean, give me a break! What's the big attraction here?"

Kendra blushed. She couldn't tell Hallie the truth, that an incredibly beautiful man had come to her room the other night and begged her to stay—and that she'd agreed. She'd sound crazy.

"Come on, tell," Hallie persisted as she combed out her curly red hair. "Are things that serious with Neil? Again? You two have been on and off for years. What's so special now, that you'd turn down two semesters of total freedom?"

"Just a feeling—I don't really know," Kendra said finally. She avoided her friend's eyes, staring instead at the wet tiles around them and the blue water lapping in the pool.

"Okay. I get it. Subject closed." Hallie leaned back in the lounge chair.

"Do you want me to read you the latest letter from Michel? He asks about you," Kendra said.

"Is it in French?"

"Of course. He writes in French; I answer in English. It's great practice for both of us."

Michel Lamont was one of the two French guys Kendra and Hallie had met several months ago at the Museum of Modern Art. Hallie hadn't kept up her correspondence with the other one, Jean-Louis, but Kendra enjoyed exchanging letters with Michel. She especially liked to hear about life in Paris, where Michel lived. For a moment, she felt a twinge of regret that she had passed up a chance to go to Europe, but it passed quickly.

"Will you translate for me?" Hallie asked as Kendra reached into the pocket of her robe for the letter.

"No way. Your French is good enough. You're just being lazy."

"That's one of the things I do best. Never mind Michel's letter. Who's coming over later? Everyone?"

Kendra nodded, then grinned as she noticed her friend hesitate.

"Go ahead," she coaxed Hallie. "I know you're dying to ask."

"Well, when is he coming back?"

"Who?" Kendra teased.

"Forget it."

"Okay, okay. I'm just kidding. My gorgeous stepbrother, Anthony, should be home from his trip to Alaska this week."

Hallie smiled with satisfaction. "I can't wait. Promise to invite me over first, before you ask any other female to come over. It's my only chance to get him to pay attention to me."

"It's a deal," Kendra told her. "You want to race some more?"

Hallie stretched and yawned. "Sure. You go ahead and start without me. Let me know when you're about to win so I can jump in ahead of you and beat you for once."

Kendra nodded and laughed as she stood up and walked around to the deep end of the pool. Hallie's great personality was one of the things Kendra loved most about her friend.

✦ ✦ ✦

"You'll write to me every week, Kennie?" Lauren said.

"Promise."

"And I'll call every Sunday."

"You're going to be too busy to call," Kendra reminded her sister. "Probably even too busy to read my letters. You'll have a great time."

"I'll miss you so much!" Lauren flung her arms around Kendra.

I'll miss you more, Kendra thought. Even though she and Lauren had had some problems in the past year, there was no one Kendra felt closer to. She couldn't believe the rest of the summer had passed so quickly, and now it was time for Lauren to leave for Switzerland. She loved Lauren more than anyone else in the world. This would be the longest they had ever been apart, and Kendra knew the separation would be painful. But she had continued to encourage Lauren to go away, even when her sister had momentary doubts. She didn't want Lauren to miss this opportunity. And, for some reason, part of her felt that Lauren would be safer farther away.

Kendra hugged Lauren and wiped away a tear before walking her downstairs.

They had already said goodbye upstairs in Lauren's room. But now they were hugging again, tearfully, as they stood in the driveway next to the open door of the car.

Dinah and Graham were taking Lauren to Switzerland. They'd make sure she was settled at school and then take a short vacation driving through the lake country. Kendra would stay with Mrs. Stavros, the housekeeper, until Anthony returned. Kendra wasn't thrilled about that arrangement. Even though Mrs. Stavros had never been unkind to Kendra, she wasn't exactly the warmest person in the world. From the first day Kendra and her family had moved into Graham's house, something about Miss Stavros had made Kendra uneasy. Still, it would only be a few days before Anthony came home.

Tears gathered in Kendra's eyes as she watched them all pile into the limo that would take them to the airport. She waved and called goodbye until the car turned a curve in the driveway and was out of sight.

If Kendra felt lonely, Max felt even worse. His tail drooped, he whined and whimpered and roamed from room to room looking for everyone, especially Lauren. The first few nights Lauren was gone, he slept by her bed, waiting. When she didn't return after a few days, Max nosed open the door to Kendra's room and flopped down on the floor. She didn't have the heart to turn him out. And, she had to admit, she liked the company.

"This is just a temporary arrangement, Max," she told the dog as she patted him on the head before turning off the lights. "When Anthony gets back, you'll have to crash with him. Sorry, but you snore."

Several days later, Kendra awoke to the sound of ecstatic barking coming from outside. She looked out the window. The tall, exceptionally cute guy with the duffel bag standing at the foot of the front steps was laughing so hard he couldn't move. The big dog was leaping as high as he could to lick his face.

Kendra threw on her bathrobe and ran down the stairs.

"Welcome home, stranger," she called as she opened the front door.

"Thanks, Kendra," Anthony replied. "Can you please peel Max off me? It's still a little warm to be wearing a fur coat!"

Kendra called to Max, who willingly went to her side. Then she gave Anthony a quick hug.

Anthony dragged his bags into the hallway. "I hope Mrs. Stavros has pancakes for breakfast. I'm starved. I'll go wash up, and be down in a minute."

Kendra watched her stepbrother climb the stairs and disappear down the hallway. Anthony was home. And Kendra didn't know who was happier—Max or herself.

CHAPTER 4

"Aaaaeeeee!" Hallie screamed. Her cry ended in a gurgle. She disappeared with a splash in the blue water of the pool as Anthony grabbed her by the waist and pulled her under.

Kendra smiled through a mouthful of water and kept swimming her laps. She enjoyed listening to Hallie and Anthony horsing around. There were only a few days left of summer vacation before school started, and she planned to spend almost every free moment of those days with Hallie and Anthony and a few other friends. She hated to see their afternoons of swimming and tennis end. But a part of her was eager to get back to classes.

Hallie popped up out of the water again, sputtering. By then, Anthony had reached the deep end of the pool and was chinning himself underneath the diving board.

"You could have drowned me!" Hallie cried, pretending to be angry. In fact, she was enjoying every minute of Anthony's attention.

"Not me," he said, grinning. "It was the sharks. The pool's full of them. Watch out! Here comes another one." He let go of the diving board and raced toward Hallie with powerful strokes.

"No!" she shrieked with delight.

He grabbed her and dunked her again.

Kendra climbed out of the pool and watched the two of them splashing around. For Hallie, spending this much time with Anthony was a dream come true—even though she understood he was mostly interested in her as a friend, not a girlfriend. Hallie would be thrilled if this summer never ended.

✦ ✦ ✦

On the first day of school, Kendra was excited about the start of the new semester. She had carefully picked out her clothes—new black miniskirt, black tennis shoes, and a black-and-white striped T-shirt, which she knew looked good with her long dark hair and summer tan. She already had a stack of brand-new notebooks for her classes. Kendra had always been a good student, and she didn't want this year to be an exception. She was especially eager to get back to the TV workshop.

When she walked into the TV studio for the last period of the day, Neil was already there. He called to her. She stepped carefully around the wires and unused lamps that clogged the control booth and joined him at one of the monitors.

"What do you think of the new set?" he asked. The broadcast area on the other side of the soundproof glass had been rebuilt during the summer. The new set looked much more professional in the greenish light of the monitor.

"Cool," she said. As she bent closer to the monitor, she felt Neil casually drape his arm around her shoulders. Without meaning to, she jumped slightly and pulled away.

"I want to ask Mr. Taylor something," she said stiffly. "See you later." She slipped out from under Neil's arm and headed for their instructor on the other side of the control booth. She didn't miss the pained expression that crossed Neil's face.

Kendra hadn't meant to hurt him. She just wanted a little space. She didn't know how to change the fact that she felt differently about him lately. In fact, she felt nothing. Neil seemed so— young. So uninteresting. There were no sparks between her and Neil anymore. What had ever attracted her to him in the first place? Ever since Revell had appeared in her room, she couldn't stop thinking about him—about his golden hair and piercing blue eyes. She could almost feel the way he had caressed her face that night. She knew she was acting cold and distant toward Neil, but she couldn't help it. All she could think about was Revell.

After the workshop ended, Kendra quickly packed up her books and headed out of the studio. She hurried in order to avoid Neil. But she could feel him staring after her with a puzzled look. She rushed to her locker and was about to grab her jacket when Hallie came up behind her.

"Want to go see a movie this afternoon?" Hallie asked. "I don't know about you, but I have hardly any homework yet. I want to enjoy my freedom while it lasts."

"Sure," Kendra agreed. They decided on a movie they both wanted to see and agreed to meet at the theater an hour later.

At home, Kendra ran up the stairs to drop off her books and brush her hair before meeting Hallie. As she headed into her bedroom, she heard noises in Lauren's room. A drawer slammed shut; then the sound of running water came from her sister's bathroom.

Kendra rushed across the hall and pushed open the door to the room. A large suitcase was open on the bed.

"Lauren?" she called. Something must have happened to make Lauren come home so soon. Something awful. "Lauren?" she called again, fearfully.

A very pretty girl stepped out of the bathroom, drying her face on a fluffy towel.

"Oh, hello. You must be Kendra. I'm Ariane Belloche," she said with a French accent. "I've been looking forward to meeting you." She held out a slim hand.

Kendra took it, trying to smile. She was actually too shocked to speak.

What was this stranger doing in Lauren's room?

"I imagine Uncle Graham and Dinah told you about me," Ariane said.

Uncle? Graham?

"I'm so happy to be here," Ariane said. "I was thrilled when Graham invited me. He is one of my very favorite people." Her English was perfect, and her accent made it sound like music. "I hope you and I will get to be good friends, Kendra. My uncle has told me so much about you."

"I—uh, welcome." Kendra couldn't help staring. Ariane wasn't just pretty—she was stunning, in a quiet, sophisticated way. Her shiny light brown hair was cut short and shaped sleekly around her head. Her brown eyes were warm and huge. She was smaller than Kendra, almost dainty, and beautifully dressed. The short, beige wool tunic she wore over a long-sleeved white blouse fit her perfectly, and her white tights showed off her shapely legs.

"Oh, you do look surprised!" Ariane said, suddenly realizing that Kendra was staring at her. "Weren't you expecting me today? Uncle Graham said he called your mother from Paris to let her know when we'd arrive."

What in the world?

Dinah had arrived home last week while Graham stayed on visiting relatives in Paris. But neither one of them had said anything about a guest.

Kendra recovered enough to be polite. "I'm really pleased to meet you, Ariane. Actually, we weren't expecting you till tomorrow," she lied. She looked around Lauren's room. "How was your trip? Do you have everything you need?"

"Yes, thank you. Mrs. Stavros has been very considerate."

Mrs. Stavros? Considerate? This was another surprise. The housekeeper was efficient and hard-working, but Kendra would never have described her as considerate.

"Excuse me, Kendra, but you look as if you were going someplace in a hurry. Please, don't let me keep you. I'm sure we'll have plenty of time to talk later. After all, I will be here for a whole year."

A year? Kendra couldn't believe it. She struggled to be courteous despite her total astonishment and confusion.

"I was just going to a movie with a friend," she explained. "You're welcome to join us—or I can change my plans. I'd be glad to help you unpack."

"That's very kind. But thank you, no. I wouldn't want to interfere. I am a little tired after the flight, anyhow—and tomorrow will be such a big day for me. I'll be going to Wilbraham Academy for the school year, starting tomorrow. Graham said that you and I are the same age and that I'd probably be in many of your classes. So you don't have to change your plans for my sake. I'll have plenty of chances to meet your friends some other day. I'm looking forward to that, too."

"Okay. See you later." Kendra gave Ariane a weak smile and headed back to her own room.

Why hadn't anyone told her about Ariane? Did Anthony know? Had Dinah bothered to tell him?

Ariane seemed perfectly nice, but still Kendra was shocked. A year was a very long time for a guest to stay. And Ariane was going to be in Kendra's school, in the same classes, all that time. What were Dinah and Graham thinking of when they invited her? Kendra had to know—right away. She finished brushing her hair and rushed downstairs.

✦ ✦ ✦

"How could you forget to tell me?" Kendra demanded. She had cornered Dinah in her study. She was glaring as she leaned over her mother's desk.

"I wish you wouldn't get so excited, darling," Dinah said, playing with the large bow of her silky blouse. "It just slipped my mind—with all the arrangements for Lauren, and our trip, and everything. Why are you so upset? What difference does it make? Ariane Belloche is a lovely girl, from a fine family in Paris, and very well brought up, Graham tells me."

"I hate surprises," Kendra said.

"Well, actually, it was a bit of a surprise to me, too. I had no idea that Ariane was so special to

Graham. He just mentioned her once, and I didn't think anything of it. In fact, I forgot all about her until he introduced us in Paris. But it's obvious how much they love each other. They're really so charming together. Such affection, even though he's not her real uncle. Actually, it's amazing that they are so very close, considering that Graham is her uncle only by marriage. Ariane is really Helen's niece."

"Helen?" Kendra echoed.

"Now, you know perfectly well who she is—well, was."

Kendra nodded. Helen had been Graham's second wife. He had married her after his first wife, Anthony's mother, died. Helen and Graham's daughter, Syrie, had also died—in a tragic crash of Graham's private plane. They were both buried in the family cemetery in a corner of the grounds of the house.

"I think Graham's idea to invite Ariane here was just perfect," Dinah continued. "With Lauren away, he said we should have some 'fresh blood' in the house. Such an odd way to put it, don't you think? But he was absolutely right. She's a darling girl. So I can't understand why you're making such a fuss." Dinah fluffed up the silky bow of her blouse and picked up some papers from her desk. She was satisfied that everything was all settled. "Ariane is here for the school year, and I hope you'll make her feel welcome."

"You know I will. I just don't like coming home and finding that a strange person has moved into Lauren's room—without a word of warning."

"You should learn to expect the unexpected, Kendra." Dinah laughed at what she thought was a terribly witty remark.

"Oh, please!"

"You'll see. You and Ariane will get along wonderfully well. I'm sure of it."

✦ ✦ ✦

For once, Kendra had to admit that Dinah was right. She couldn't help but like Ariane. And all of Kendra's friends at Wilbraham liked Ariane, too.

Ariane was very sociable, and she had terrific taste. Kendra's girlfriends started asking Ariane for advice about clothes and makeup. She was always glad to help, without seeming smug or superior. And the guys fell all over her—especially Anthony, who hadn't seen her since they were very young.

"Weren't you ever curious about Ariane?" Kendra asked Anthony.

"Not really," he said. "I was too young when my mother died and Graham married Helen. I never thought about Helen's family in Europe. They weren't my real relatives, after all. I only met Ariane and her mother once when they visited New York. And Graham never took me to Paris when he and Helen traveled there after Syrie was born. I was always away at boarding school or summer camp when they took their trips."

"But when you were growing up, didn't you ever wonder about Ariane? After all, she and Graham are so close. He must have talked about her."

"No, he never did. I guess it is surprising. I feel like I'm meeting someone for the first time and finding out that she's been a part of my life almost forever. Now that I see her, I'd like to know more about these unrelated relatives. Maybe I'll check them out." A shy smile came over his face. "She's really awesome, isn't she?"

"Yeah," Kendra agreed halfheartedly. It was obvious that Anthony really liked Ariane.

In fact, everyone was crazy about Ariane— except Max.

One afternoon, Kendra, Ariane, Hallie, and Judy Matthews, another of Kendra's friends from school, were hanging out in Kendra's room. They were checking out some of the makeup that Ariane had brought from Paris.

"Totally excellent!" Hallie said, admiring a bright pink lipstick.

"I think I've got the same shade or something like it," Kendra said. She went to her dresser to find it. "That's odd," she said, poking around in the back of a drawer. "I was sure I put it here." But the lipstick was gone. As she searched, she didn't see Max nose open the door and come looking for her. All of a sudden, Kendra heard a rumbling snarl, a growl that came deep from the animal's throat. And then a bewildered, terrified cry.

Kendra whirled around to see Ariane cowering in the corner. Max was planted in front of her. The hairs on his back stood up, and he faced the frightened girl as if he might attack.

"Max!" Kendra cried.

He began to bark furiously, not even looking at Kendra. Kendra couldn't believe it. She'd never seen Max act so aggressively.

"Max! No!"

The big black dog backed away and slunk to Kendra's side, whimpering.

"Shame on you! What's gotten into you? Out! Come on, scram!"

Kendra grabbed his collar and led him to the door. She watched as he thumped down the stairs. It seemed that every part of his big body drooped. Something about Ariane had spooked him. Kendra realized that Max had been behaving strangely around Ariane ever since she arrived. What was it about her that frightened the usually friendly dog? It was something bad enough to make him threaten her. And it made Kendra uneasy. Is there really something wrong about Ariane? she wondered.

When Kendra returned to her room, Ariane looked pale but was trying to behave as if nothing unusual had happened. Kendra noticed that Ariane's hand was shaking as she reached into her makeup bag and pulled out a long wand of dark mascara with silver sparkles. Ariane had been badly frightened.

While Ariane and Judy stood in front of the mirror, applying mascara to their lashes, Hallie shot Kendra a questioning look. Max had never behaved like that before, and Hallie knew it as well as Kendra did. Kendra shook her head and shrugged in response.

Later Kendra took Ariane aside. "Sorry about Max," she said. "I don't know what got into him."

"It was nothing, really," Ariane said lightly. "I've always been a little afraid of dogs, ever since I was a child. Maybe he sensed it. Like horses. They always know when you're scared of them."

Nothing more was said about the incident. Still it bothered Kendra. Why had Max acted so oddly? Just to be on the safe side, Kendra banished him from her room—and from the entire third floor.

✦ ✦ ✦

"Hi, Ken," Anthony greeted her as she came down the stairs. "Have you seen Ariane?"

Kendra couldn't help feeling a bit offended. It seemed as though no one could talk to her anymore without mentioning Ariane.

"Want to try that again?" Kendra snapped. "How about, 'Hello, Ken, and how are you today? Looking great, I see.'"

He smiled. "That's what I meant to say."

"I knew it," she replied with a grin. "I haven't seen Ariane."

They walked together through the great marble front hall into the huge main living room. It was empty.

"She's not here," Kendra said.

"We were going to play tennis this afternoon. She isn't out at the court. I checked."

"You just like to play with her because you can beat her so easily."

Anthony shrugged. "I'm only trying to make her feel at home."

"I know." Kendra smiled. "I don't mean to tease you. You really like Ariane, don't you?"

He smiled sheepishly.

"I'm glad," Kendra added quickly. "She's really nice. And after what happened with Max, I'm sure she loves having someone look out for her."

Anthony looked at her, puzzled. When she explained Max's behavior the other day, he just laughed.

"I'm sure Max was only playing. He'd never attack someone who was welcome in our home. Not ever."

"Okay, so we're just a bunch of silly girls imagining stuff," Kendra said indignantly. "Too bad you weren't there."

Anthony raised his eyebrows at Kendra's sharp tone. "You're right. I didn't see what happened," he said. "But I can't imagine Max acting that way."

Kendra shrugged and let the subject drop. "Why don't you try the court again?" she suggested. "Maybe Ariane went out through the back, and you missed each other. I'll keep looking. If I find her, I'll send her out for her next lesson in how to lose gracefully."

"Thanks," Anthony said. He waved one of his rackets and headed for the tennis court.

Kendra continued wandering through the main floor, looking for Ariane. She enjoyed going from room to room in the spacious old mansion. She peered into her mother's study and Graham's library. But there was no sign of Ariane.

At last, she gave up and headed for the kitchen to get a glass of juice.

She pushed open the kitchen door. At first, she thought the big white-and-blue-tiled room was empty. Then she saw the two of them in the corner near the pantry. Whispering together. Ariane and Mrs. Stavros.

"There you are!" Kendra called. "Anthony's been looking for you, Ariane. He's out at the . . . . "

Ariane and Mrs. Stavros broke off their conversation abruptly and looked at Kendra. Their expressions were so peculiar that she couldn't even finish her sentence.

They act as if I'm an intruder!

They didn't say anything. They just stared coldly at her.

Kendra's temper suddenly flared out of control.

This is my home! How dare they make me feel I don't belong here?

Without warning, a large saucepan that was

sitting on the stove began to boil over, hissing and steaming in an oozing red mess—like blood!—all over the stove, over the floor. It was as if the pot was spilling over with Kendra's own anger.

All three of them were shocked at the sight.

Mrs. Stavros rushed to control the damage. "The fire was off under that pot," she said as she ran to the stove. "I know I turned it off!" Ariane slipped through the pantry door and disappeared outside.

What did I interrupt? Kendra wondered angrily as she poured herself the glass of juice she had come for. What were Mrs. Stavros and Ariane whispering about? And why did they look so guilty when I walked in?

✦ ✦ ✦

Later, Kendra thought about Mrs. Stavros. The housekeeper had changed ever since her husband had died so gruesomely months ago. Kendra recalled fondly how Mr. Stavros took such good care of the gardens. She remembered how horrified she was when she saw him lying on the ground, a pair of hedge clippers piercing his chest.

Since then, Mrs. Stavros had been even quieter than before. The expression on her face was gloomier, and her thoughts always seemed to be far away. Kendra assumed she was still in mourning and suffering deeply from the loss of Mr. Stavros. But lately, since Ariane's arrival, Mrs. Stavros appeared more cheerful. She seemed happy to do special things for the French girl. And when Kendra saw them together in the kitchen, they actually looked as if they were in a conspiracy. What was going on between them?

Kendra wondered about Ariane, too. There was definitely something strange about her. Kendra decided she would keep an eye on Ariane.

CHAPTER 5

"... And don't forget, Kennie, you promised you'd check on Vinnie. Give him a hug from me, and an apple, and if he looks really sad, just a little bite of a Twinkie. ..."

Kendra chuckled at Lauren's latest letter.

She was sitting on a bench in the old family cemetery on the grounds of the mansion. To her surprise, she didn't find the graveyard gruesome at all. Ever since she had moved in, she felt drawn to the spot. Giant trees, hundreds of years old, surrounded the quiet, peaceful cemetery, blocking the sunlight from filtering through. Kendra felt most serene when she glanced out at the rows of white tombstones. It was as if she had a kinship, weird and baffling, with all those lying dead beneath her feet.

For some reason, Kendra especially liked to sit near the graves of Graham's second wife, Helen, and their daughter, Syrie. She couldn't help feeling a special bond with the tragic girl.

Syrie. Her name was so lovely. To Kendra, it sounded like wind through the trees, like music.

She put Lauren's letter down for a minute and studied Syrie's tombstone. She had read the dates of her birth and death many times before and was always moved to tears. Syrie and her mother had been killed in a plane crash when Syrie was only seventeen—the same age Kendra was now.

A strange thought distracted her. Syrie was seventeen. I'm seventeen. And so is Ariane. How many others . . .? Her eyes roamed over the many grave markers stretched out around her. She shivered. She knew that most of the graves held the bodies of girls who had died at age seventeen. Does life here freeze at age seventeen? Kendra wondered. Or something worse?

But I'm alive, and Syrie is . . . .

She looked at Syrie's grave again. It was bizarre how strangely close Kendra felt to this girl she had never met.

On a sudden impulse, she leaned toward the stone.

"Syrie?" she whispered gently.

A breeze rose throughout the graveyard. The leaves on the trees rustled and said, "Ssshhhh."

Then Kendra felt the air go cold around her. A dark sensation of fear gripped her. What was happening? Something dangerous hovered in the air, so close Kendra could feel it. She shivered and tried to ignore the feeling. She picked up Lauren's letter again.

". . . I'm getting used to not having guys around at school. But some of the ski instructors are H-U-N-Ks! They make Anthony and Neil look like dweebs. Just kidding! Most of the girls are real cool. One of my best friends is Mumtaz—cool name, isn't it? She's from India and her hair is so long she can sit on it!"

A low moan rose in the air.

What was that sound? Did someone call my name?

Kendra looked around. She was alone. The moaning stopped.

She continued reading to the end of Lauren's letter:

"I miss you like crazy. If you're sad because you miss me, you can have the other half of Vinnie's Twinkie. Love—love—love!!!"

She tucked the letter into her pocket. She would answer Lauren tonight. She pulled out the letter she had just received from Michel in Paris. The last time she wrote to him, she had mentioned Ariane's coming to stay.

To her surprise, Michel's letter said that he knew Ariane slightly. She was a friend of a classmate of his. Michel said he didn't like to gossip, but he knew that Ariane had had some trouble in Paris last year. He was glad she'd been able to get away to New York for a while.

What kind of trouble? Kendra wondered. Ariane seemed so sweet and innocent. Maybe Kendra wasn't reading Michel's French correctly.

She folded the letter and stood up. She would go back to the house and check her French dictionary.

As she turned to leave the cemetery, she saw a strange light hovering over Syrie's tombstone. She looked around, trying to figure out what was causing the glow.

When Kendra looked at the stone again, it was the same as always.

She sighed and told herself her imagination was running away with her.

✦ ✦ ✦

That's weird. I know I put them here.

Kendra was looking for the small bundle of letters from Michel so she could include his most recent one about Ariane with the others. She had tucked the bundle into a drawer in her desk, way in the back.

For a moment, she thought she had put them somewhere else. No, she was sure that was where she'd left them, in her desk drawer. Then she remembered the missing lipstick the other day. Was someone moving her things? Taking them? What was going on?

Ariane.

The name popped into her head. Who else would be going through her things? Certainly not

Dinah, or Anthony, or Graham. It had to be Ariane—but why? Why would Ariane be snooping through Kendra's things? Kendra didn't want to mistrust Ariane, but she was growing very uncomfortable about their house guest. There were too many unanswered questions about her.

For one thing, why had Ariane left Paris and come to New York? There was something bizarre about the way she had just shown up that day in Lauren's room, no matter how easily Dinah explained it away. And what had Ariane been whispering about with Mrs. Stavros? Kendra was positive it had been something to do with her.

Kendra sat down on her bed, considering the situation. Finally, she decided there was no point in turning into a nut case about a missing lipstick and some unimportant letters. Maybe Kendra had simply misplaced them. They would probably turn up somewhere.

She decided to hide Michel's latest letter in the pocket of her oldest ski jacket in the back of her closet and keep her suspicions about Ariane to herself.

A few days later, Kendra couldn't find her science notebook. Her doubts about Ariane came rushing back. This time Kendra was absolutely sure where she had left her notebook—in a stack of school books on top of her dresser. Now it was gone.

"Ariane!" Kendra crossed the hall to Lauren's room. She would confront Ariane right now.

But Ariane wasn't there. Kendra would have to wait.

Or would she . . .?

Kendra started searching the room. She didn't have to look far. Her missing science notebook was in the middle desk drawer with the rest of Ariane's school books.

Kendra snatched her notebook out of the drawer and stood there, stunned for a moment. Why was Ariane taking her things? She started to leave the room, then hesitated. What else of hers might Ariane be hiding?

Nervously, Kendra returned to the desk and started looking through the other drawers. When she didn't find anything else of hers in the desk, she turned to the dresser and opened the top drawer. She began to feel uncomfortable. She was about to close the drawer and leave the room when she heard a noise in the doorway.

"What are you doing?" Ariane asked in a soft voice.

Kendra spun around. She could feel her face turn flame red.

"You took my notebook out of my room," she stated, sounding flustered. "I came in to find it."

Now it was Ariane's turn to blush. She came into the bedroom, her eyelids fluttering with shame. She looked at the notebook in Kendra's hand, then burst out in a shaky voice.

"Oh, please forgive me! I—I didn't mean . . . I'm

so sorry! You are so much better in science. I wanted to borrow your notes."

"So you just went into my room and took them?"

"I meant to ask, b-but you weren't home."

"You have no right to go through my things. Not for any reason!" Kendra snapped. She surprised herself with the sudden force of her anger. It was as if she could no longer contain her growing mistrust of Ariane. "Don't ever go into my room again when I'm not there!" she exploded. "And don't touch anything of mine again—not ever!"

Ariane's eyes filled with tears.

"I only w-wanted to study. It's hard for me to keep up. Science is very difficult. It's important. I must do well at school."

The tears spilled over. Ariane looked so miserable that Kendra found herself feeling sorry for the girl. And Ariane's story sounded so convincing, Kendra couldn't stay angry.

"Forget it," Kendra said, her tone softening.

"No. I know how angry you are. I don't blame you. I shouldn't have gone into your room."

"Don't worry about it, Ariane. It's okay."

"I feel so terrible. I wanted us to be f-friends." Ariane was sobbing.

"We are friends," Kendra reassured her. "I'll help you with your science homework anytime. And you can borrow my notes whenever you like. Just ask next time. Okay?"

Ariane sniffled and blew her nose. She nodded and smiled with relief.

Kendra left Ariane's room with a pang of regret. She hadn't meant to upset Ariane like that.

Wow, did you fly off the handle! she scolded herself. She only borrowed your notebook, and you immediately assumed she's responsible for taking everything else you've misplaced.

As Kendra headed back to her room, she reminded herself that Ariane was still new in town and far away from her family and friends. No wonder she had burst into tears when Kendra yelled at her.

Kendra sat down at her desk with the notebook and flipped it open. But as she searched through the pages for her notes on genetics, the birthmark on her hand began to tingle again.

She frowned and rubbed the spot thoughtfully.

Was this some kind of warning about Ariane?

CHAPTER 6

Neil Jarmon stared at the shiny red object in Kendra's hand.

"Lauren sent it from Switzerland?" he asked. "Why did she bother? You can buy a dozen like it right here in New York."

"Nope, this one is special." She laughed. "At least, Lauren thinks it is. It's a genuine, officially official Swiss Army knife from Switzerland. With about thirty tools and blades that pop out on all sides. Look, it's even got something for scaling fish."

"Yeah, I noticed you've been having trouble managing without a fish scaler for years."

Kendra laughed, partly because she was relieved that Neil had gotten over being hurt and that they were still friends. She knew he hoped that they could continue dating. But she would cope with that when she had to.

They were having lunch at the Mad Deli on Madison Avenue between classes. It was the first time Kendra had felt like going back there since their classmate Rob Prentis had almost choked to death at her table last semester. She still shuddered thinking about it.

Neil leaned across the table, studying the knife. "Are you sure you ought to bring something like that to school?"

"It's okay." Kendra put the knife back into her bag. "I'm going to hide it in my locker. I feel it's really special because Lauren sent it to me. I don't want to keep it in my room at home."

"Why not?" Neil asked.

Because I can't bear the thought that Ariane might take it. At the thought of Ariane, Kendra's bright mood darkened.

"You look upset," Neil said. "Is something wrong?"

Kendra didn't know how to answer. She was afraid that her fears might sound silly, but she didn't want to lie to Neil. Especially not now when they were getting along better.

"It's nothing," Kendra said. "At least, it's probably nothing. Lately, I've noticed that some of my things have been disappearing."

"Like what? What are you talking about?" Neil sounded confused.

"Well, first, it was just small things. A lipstick, then some letters and other stuff, like clothes and school books. But this morning, I noticed that my bracelet is missing."

"The one Graham gave you?" Neil asked.

Kendra nodded. Graham had given her the bracelet shortly after she had moved into the mansion. It was a beautiful, delicate gold circle studded with blood-red garnets. It had belonged to Graham's daughter, Syrie. Kendra felt a little weird about wearing it, but she had become attached to it. In a strange way, she was drawn to everything about the dead girl's life. She felt there was an invisible connection between her and Syrie, one she didn't fully understand. Just as she couldn't understand her feelings about Ariane.

"You think someone's been stealing your things?" Neil said.

"Ariane," Kendra said sadly.

"No! I mean, she's so nice. I can't picture her going into your room and taking your stuff."

"I don't know who else could be doing it," Kendra said gloomily. "It's certainly not Dinah or my stepfather. Or Anthony. And Mrs. Stavros has worked for Graham for years. She might be a grouch, but I'm sure she wouldn't steal."

Neil shook his head in disbelief. "I think you should lighten up, Ken. Just because you misplaced a couple of things doesn't mean Ariane's a thief. Besides, she really thinks you're the coolest. She'd never mess around with your stuff. I don't think she'd risk doing anything to make you mad."

Kendra sighed and let the subject drop. Neil thought she was crazy. That was why she hadn't told Dinah or Graham about her missing things yet. They'd blame Kendra, too. Her conversation with Neil had only proved that she needed to be more careful about what she said about Ariane to other people. Until she had some solid evidence.

✦ ✦ ✦

That night Kendra groaned in her sleep.

"Revell . . .?" she mumbled.

She was dreaming in bright splashes of color—gold and electric blue—and sparkling lights. Something was hidden inside the riot of color and light, but she couldn't see what it was.

The tinkling of crystal chimes woke her. The sparkling fireflies of her dream swirled around her room.

"I'm here, my love," a voice said softly.

Kendra sat up, rubbing her eyes. She wasn't dreaming. He had really come to her again.

"Revell?"

Slowly, he stepped out of the whirling lights. The glow of his golden hair seemed to illuminate the whole room. He came close to the bed and smiled down at her.

Kendra smiled with pleasure. She was thrilled to see him.

"You called to me in your dreams, Kendra. You've missed me, just as I've missed you."

She nodded expectantly.

"We belong together," Revell continued. "You see, I need you. Urgently."

Revell needed her?

"I—I don't understand."

He smiled at her again, sending warmth flooding through her body. He leaned down and touched her lips lightly. "Have you been losing things lately?"

Now Kendra was more confused. How did he know about her missing things?

Revell seemed to read her thoughts. "I know everything about you, Kendra. Even when we're apart, I'm with you." He stared into her eyes. "Syrie's bracelet means a lot to you. You can punish the thief, you know. You can send Ariane away. Far away, where she'll never trouble anyone. You can get rid of her forever, if you hate her."

Kendra shook her head. "I don't hate anyone. And even if Ariane is the thief, how could I possibly make her leave? She's Graham's niece. He invited her here."

Revell caressed her cheek. "You can do almost anything you want, Kendra. You are a Sensitive, a brilliant one."

"What? A Sensitive? What are you talking about?"

"The Sensitives—the special ones, those with extraordinary powers. Gifted girls just like you, born at the last stroke of midnight. There are many Sensitives in this world, all born with the ability to control the life around them. You have this gift,

Kendra. You have even the powers of life and death at your command."

Kendra could barely take in his words. "That sounds awful," she exclaimed. "I don't want any powers like that!"

"Well, you have them. And you've used them before."

She thought for a second, then gasped.

"Neil?"

"Yes, you saved his life. That was your doing."

Kendra closed her eyes. She remembered the strange way the ground had given way under Neil's feet, his long, treacherous tumble down the cliff . . . then the abrupt halt. She had stopped him? She had prevented his death?

If what Revell was saying was true—that she did have extraordinary powers—maybe she was also responsible for harming Neil. Had she caused his fall off the cliff?

Or had Revell?

Her eyes fluttered open. She stared blankly at Revell's face.

"You saved him, Kendra," he said softly, his eyes piercing hers. "You have the power."

A flicker of fear passed through Kendra. She was confused and afraid.

Revell smiled confidently. "I told you, I need you. You are strong, Kendra. You are the Sensitive who will give me eternal life. Nothing will stop me from doing whatever I must to be with you."

Eternal life? She shook her head. This was all too much for her to understand. "Why me? If there are other—what did you call us?—other Sensitives, why not one of them?"

"Because no one has ever been as strong as you. Your strength will grow. It will keep me alive. One day you will join me in another world, in a life more beautiful than you can ever imagine."

"What—what life?"

"A better life. In a world of beauty and love, where there is no death."

Kendra's mind was reeling. She backed away from him. What exactly did he want from her?

"We will be so happy together, Kendra. I am your destiny. We are meant to be together. And you know it." His voice murmured softly, soothing her like water flowing over pebbles in a brook.

Kendra felt her fears slowly fading. She was overcome by a desire to be close to him—to be a part of his life.

He reached out for her. "Take my hand, Kendra. Come closer. Look into my eyes."

Almost without realizing it, Kendra met his gaze. Those eyes. Electric blue and sparkling. They were so deep. She felt as if she were drowning inside them. Revell opened his arms to wrap them around her. She was helpless to stop herself. She moved eagerly into his embrace, hungry to feel him hold her. How safe and happy she felt!

"Kendra," he breathed her name into her hair. "You are so beautiful. I will keep you safe. You'll never want us to part again."

"Oh, yes," she whispered.

Revell's lips found hers. As he kissed her, she clung to him tightly, desperately. She had never felt such longing for anyone.

Silently, after a long while, he slipped from her embrace.

The firefly lights closed in around him.

Suddenly, her room felt cold and empty. A sharp pain pierced Kendra's heart. Revell was gone. And she missed him more than she could believe.

CHAPTER 7

The morning after Revell's visit, Kendra woke up later than usual. She felt rested, as if she had been sleeping for days. She lay in bed for a few extra minutes, unwilling to make herself get up. Had Revell's appearance the night before been just a dream?

No, Kendra told herself. It had been real, very real. She could still feel the thrill of his arms around her and his full lips brushing hers. She missed him so much her heart ached. And the worst part was not knowing when—or if—he would return.

The persistent beeping of her clock radio finally forced Kendra up and out of bed. She jumped into the shower and dressed quickly. Then she hurried downstairs to grab a fast breakfast before school.

Mrs. Stavros was serving pancakes to Graham and Anthony. Graham was pouring himself a cup of coffee, and Anthony was trying desperately to keep his eyes open.

Graham smiled at Kendra and said, "Good morning."

"Morning," Anthony added sleepily. "Ready for your killer math test?"

Kendra just grumbled in response as she helped herself to juice and a pancake.

Anthony raised his eyebrows. "We're in a good mood, I see."

Kendra shot him a warning look. All she wanted today was to be left alone with her thoughts. Not only did she miss Revell with a force that almost overwhelmed her, she was worried about what he had told her last night. Did she really have powers? Could she really save—or harm—people simply by willing it?

Anthony wolfed down his pancakes, then stood up. "See you later, Kendra."

Kendra nodded. A minute later, she put down her fork and gathered up her books. She said goodbye to Graham and headed out the door. As she hurried onto the street, she was wondering when she would ever find out the answers to all the questions spinning around her head.

✦ ✦ ✦

For the rest of the week, Kendra kept to herself. Revell hadn't returned. And so far, to her relief, she hadn't seen any new sign of her supposed powers. Maybe Revell was just a dream.

On Friday night, she was relaxing in the living room with Dinah and Graham. She had just opened a magazine when Neil called. He invited her over to watch a videotape. She turned him down, saying she felt like staying home and reading instead.

"What's up with you, Ken?" Neil asked softly. "The other day, I thought we were getting along better. Now you're like ice again. Don't you want to go out with me anymore?"

"I do," Kendra began, fumbling for words. "It's just—"

"Just what?" Neil pressed her. "You've been so strange lately. And really moody. Sometimes you're friendly, but then, when I try to get close, you turn cold. I don't get it."

"I don't either," she answered truthfully. "I guess you're right. I really don't know why I'm acting this way."

"You haven't met someone else, have you?" Neil asked. "Someone at school?"

Kendra hesitated. "No, that's not it," she said finally. "I just need some space—or something."

Neil was silent for a minute. "Okay," he said. "Take all the space you want."

There was a click in Kendra's ear as he hung up the receiver.

Kendra sat holding the phone for a moment, surprised. She was sorry that she had hurt Neil. But she couldn't help herself. The truth was, she didn't feel very interested in him these days, and she couldn't easily pretend otherwise. Still, he didn't have to hang up on me like that, she thought angrily.

With a sigh, Kendra wandered back into the living room and picked up her magazine again. A few minutes later, Ariane came downstairs dressed like a super-model in a simple, shimmery-gold mini that brought out the highlights in her light brown hair. A single broad band of the fabric was held by a clasp at one shoulder, and she had draped a long filmy scarf over her bare shoulder. Her makeup was so perfect it didn't look like makeup at all, except that her eyes seemed larger and as shiny as her dress.

She walked into the living room trailing the scarf and a delicious breeze of perfume.

Kendra looked up at Ariane's dress, then down at her own scruffy jeans and T-shirt. For a brief instant, Kendra felt like a toad.

"I just wanted to say goodnight," Ariane said.

"You look lovely, my dear," Dinah said.

"Thank you." Ariane leaned over the back of Graham's armchair and kissed his cheek.

"Let me see," Graham said. "Yes, very beautiful—as always. Now, not too late, Ariane," he cautioned.

"Ready?" Anthony called from the doorway of the living room. He was dressed for a night out in black pants and a new shirt.

"Where are you guys off to?" Kendra asked.

"Feathers," Anthony said. "A new club. It just

opened, and everybody is raving about it. Tonight is invitation only."

"Yes." Ariane laughed. "They invited Anthony and he invited me. I'm so excited!"

"Don't forget your keys," Graham called as they left.

After they left, Ariane's perfume still hovered in the air.

Kendra stared after them, suddenly feeling miserable about staying home.

She threw the magazine on the sofa and stood up. After a hasty goodnight to Dinah and Graham, she climbed the stairs to her room. Unable to stop herself, she peered into Ariane's room and scanned the desk and dresser for any of her belongings. Kendra didn't see anything—not that Ariane would leave something she'd stolen out in the open.

Then Kendra's eyes rested on the night stand. Ariane had propped up a framed photograph of herself and two of her friends from Paris. It was the only trace of Ariane's life in France in the room.

As she stared at the picture, Kendra found herself wondering again about Ariane's past and her sudden arrival in New York. Michel had mentioned some trouble she had had at home. What was it that caused Ariane to leave Paris so abruptly? And why had she come to live with Graham?

It seemed as if Kendra's entire life had changed suddenly since Ariane's arrival. Anthony was never around anymore, Max was acting strangely, and Kendra's things continued to disappear. Her bracelet still hadn't turned up, and Kendra had almost no doubt that Ariane had taken it.

I wish she'd just go back to Paris where she belongs, Kendra thought spitefully.

A second later, the framed photo soared off the night stand and clattered to the floor. As it hit the polished wood, the frame split wide open, and the glass panel shattered into hundreds of tiny pieces.

Kendra's hand flew over her mouth. She ran to her room without bothering to pick up the broken frame or the photo. Had she caused the picture to fall? Was this what Revell had meant when he said she had such great powers—destructive powers, even —that she could punish Ariane?

If I'm capable of doing something like that— destroying Ariane's photo—what else can I do?

She sat down heavily on her bed. She didn't want to think about what had just happened— or about her powers. But she couldn't avoid it. What was going on? Was she going to have to make sure that she never got angry at anyone again? Would something destructive like this happen every time?

If only there were someone she could confide in. Graham?

Almost as soon as his name came to mind,

Kendra rejected the idea. She loved her stepfather, but something about him made her uneasy.

His voice echoed in her mind: "You've done enough damage . . ."

Those were the words she had overheard Graham say many months ago—to someone hidden. So many things seemed to be hidden from Kendra lately. It was as if part of her memory had disappeared. Bits and pieces of memories sometimes returned, but she knew that much was still missing. And some of those missing pieces concerned Graham. She felt she couldn't—she mustn't—trust him. How could she ever expect him to believe anything she told him about Revell? And he certainly wouldn't believe her suspicions about Ariane. After all, Graham was the one who had brought her into their home.

Tears began to stream down Kendra's face. She had never felt so alone or confused in her life.

✦ ✦ ✦

Judy Matthews slammed the ball across the net. Hallie made a desperate dive for it, but missed.

They were playing doubles, Judy and Kendra against Hallie and Neil. That morning, Kendra had decided to call Neil and make up with him. Despite their argument the night before, he had sounded happy to hear her voice. And calling him had cheered Kendra up as well. Neil had been too good a friend for too long. She couldn't let that friendship end with bad feelings between them.

She didn't have to remind herself that friendship was different from love. Revell had left no room in her heart for any other man but him.

The score was even until Judy made the next two points, and Kendra and Judy won.

"What a bummer!" Hallie said. "I'm sending myself to the showers."

"Don't be discouraged," Neil said. "You've gotten much better since the summer, really."

"Want to take us on?" Judy called across the net to Neil. "You against me and Kendra?"

"I'm going upstairs with Hallie," Kendra said. "You two play alone."

"Are you crazy?" Hallie whispered as she and Kendra left the tennis court. "She'll gobble him up before you even zip up your racket."

Kendra laughed. She was used to Judy's flirting, especially with Neil. She wasn't worried. Besides, Judy was the least of the problems between her and Neil right now.

"Neil's a big boy," she told Hallie on the way up the stairs to her room. "He can take care of himself."

Hallie raised her eyebrows. "You're more trusting than I would ever be, Ken. My philosophy is, when you don't guard your possessions you can lose them."

Kendra stopped on the step above Hallie. "Why did you say that?"

"No reason." Hallie seemed surprised by her

reaction. "I just don't want Judy to make a move on Neil."

"No. I mean about losing possessions."

Hallie shrugged. "I didn't mean anything special. Why?"

"Oh, forget it." Kendra relaxed. She had to stop being suspicious about every little thing. "To the showers. You first. You did most of the sweating out there."

"So, how's it going with Ariane?" Hallie asked after they had both showered and were sitting on Kendra's bed.

"Fine," Kendra said nonchalantly. "She's got super taste, doesn't she? I've never seen such a collection of clothes outside of a magazine."

"Yeah, I drool over everything she wears. Imagine looking like a model just to go to school! Have you noticed, all the girls in our class are dressing better since she came? Too bad she's so small you can't borrow anything."

"The only thing of hers that I could fit into is her perfume," Kendra said.

Hallie smiled, then looked closely at Kendra. "Okay, what is it? Something's up, isn't it? Don't you two get along?"

"Sure we do. It's just strange, having someone in Lauren's room. Every time I hear her across the hall, I think it's Lauren."

Hallie wasn't satisfied. "That's not all of it, is it? I've been watching her, and I've been watching you. Lately, you've been acting really strange whenever someone mentions Ariane."

"That's not true!" Kendra protested. "I like her, really. Everyone likes her."

"I've noticed. The whole world is bonkers over our dear little visitor from across the sea. Anthony, especially. Am I right?"

Kendra nodded. "Sorry to break it to you, Hallie."

"Believe me, I've noticed. So you don't like Ariane?"

Kendra met her friend's eyes. "The truth?"

Hallie nodded.

"I like her—but I'm not sure I trust her."

"Me neither," Hallie responded.

"What?"

"Ariane's nice and everything," Hallie went on. "But sometimes I get the feeling she's hiding something. She never says much about her family or her friends back home, and I still don't get why she's here. I mean, you don't arrange a visit to the United States that quickly unless you need to get away from something. Know what I mean?"

Kendra threw herself across the bed and hugged her friend. She felt relieved that someone else had the same uncomfortable feeling about Ariane.

"There are a lot of unanswered questions about Ariane," Kendra said. "I think she's been stealing my things. Some makeup, my science notebook, even Michel's letters."

"I'm surprised she'd take your things," Hallie

said. "Especially *those* things. Frankly, Ken, you've got much better stuff to steal than Michel's letters."

"I think she wanted what was inside one of the letters," Kendra said. Kendra quickly filled Hallie in about what Michel had said about Ariane. "I don't know what happened in Paris, Hallie, but there's got to be a reason why Graham asked Ariane to stay for such a long time. I have some theories."

Kendra heard a noise outside her bedroom and stopped talking.

Ariane stood in the doorway, glaring at them. How long had she been there? From the look on her face, it was obvious that she had overheard every word. Her delicate features were twisted in anger, and her eyes blazed.

Kendra drew in her breath. She had been so eager to blurt out the whole story to someone, she hadn't even thought about whether Ariane was at home. How could she have been so stupid? After weeks of being careful not to reveal her true feelings around Ariane, she had just blown everything.

Burning with shame, Kendra met the other girl's eyes.

"You think you know everything about me, Kendra," Ariane said. Her voice was an ominous snarl. "You think you are so very special, don't you? The only one who is special. But you are wrong. There are many things about me you do not know. In fact, you know nothing at all."

With those words, Ariane turned on her heel and disappeared from the doorway.

Kendra and Hallie stared at each other in silence as they heard Ariane race down the stairs and slam the front door behind her.

CHAPTER 8

Graham looked up as Kendra walked into the breakfast room on Monday morning. "Well, here are the two prettiest flowers in my garden."

Kendra turned in surprise. She hadn't realized Ariane was close behind her. They hadn't spoken since Ariane had stormed out of Kendra's room Saturday afternoon. Kendra still felt bad and embarrassed about her gossiping session with Hallie.

"Good morning, Uncle Graham," Ariane said. She laughed at Graham's flattery and kissed him before she took her seat at the table. She didn't look at Kendra. She reached for a fluffy croissant, her favorite breakfast. Ever since Ariane came, Mrs. Stavros had been baking the delicate buttery rolls just to please her. Apparently, the house-keeper had fallen under Ariane's spell like everyone else.

"You're very quiet this morning, Kendra," Graham said. He watched her carefully spoon some cottage cheese onto a slice of melon. "Why so glum?"

"I'm not glum," Kendra protested. "I was just thinking about the story I prepared for my TV workshop this afternoon. There's one fact I want to double-check. I'm on camera today," she explained.

"Oh, that reminds me," Ariane said. "I spoke to Mr. Taylor and asked him if I could join the workshop. I've always been so interested in television, and Wilbraham has such a marvelous studio. Mr. Taylor accepted me, just to audit at first. I hope you don't mind, Kendra."

"Of course not," Kendra answered quickly. The truth was, she did mind—a lot. But what could she say? Besides, part of her was relieved that Ariane was speaking to her again.

Graham beamed. "What a good idea, Ariane! You'll be a star by the time you go home."

"I'll never be as good as Kendra," Ariane said sweetly. "Everyone at school talks about how professional she is on camera." She glanced quickly at Kendra. "If it bothers you, though, I can drop out."

"Nonsense!" Graham said. "Kendra would be glad to show you the ropes, I'm sure. Isn't that so?"

"Absolutely," Kendra said in a hollow voice. She smiled stiffly at Ariane and tried to pretend she didn't mind a bit.

What part of my life is Ariane going to invade

next? Kendra wondered as she closed the front door behind her and headed down the driveway.

When Kendra got to school, she double-checked her facts and gave her copy to Mr. Taylor to put on the teleprompter for the afternoon news. Then she went to her first class.

When the bell for last period rang, Kendra put her books in her locker and headed for the studio.

She entered the studio and waved to her cameraperson. She sat down on the set, straightened her skirt, and checked her hair.

Then Kendra had the feeling that someone was staring at her. She peered into the control booth and saw Ariane looking back at her. Kendra was still upset that Ariane was auditing the TV workshop, but she smiled at Ariane.

Ariane didn't smile back. She glowered at Kendra, her eyes full of anger. Then she turned to ask Mr. Taylor a question.

Kendra was shocked at Ariane's response. She became flustered and dropped her notes.

As she picked up her notes and arranged them in the proper order, Kendra tried to regain her composure.

I guess Ariane is only speaking to me when Graham is around, Kendra thought. That's fine with me.

✦ ✦ ✦

Kendra tried to avoid Ariane for the rest of the week. After Ariane had overheard her gossiping with Hallie, and the incident at the television studio, Kendra had decided to keep a low profile—at least until she had more proof that Ariane was taking her things.

Then, on Friday, as she walked in the door after school, Kendra saw Ariane and Graham talking in the living room. She couldn't help hearing the conversation as she passed the doorway.

"I'm so glad to see you wearing it, Ariane. You have no idea how that pleases me."

Kendra glanced inside the living room.

Graham was holding Ariane's hand, looking down, smiling as he touched something on her wrist.

Curious, Kendra walked into the living room for a closer look. Neither Graham nor Ariane noticed her. She stopped halfway across the room. Her mouth opened in shock.

Ariane was wearing Kendra's gold-and-garnet bracelet, the one that had been missing for weeks!

How dare she? And why is Graham so pleased to see Ariane wearing it? He gave that bracelet to me! Kendra thought. She was furious at both of them. And she couldn't stand another minute of Ariane's taking her things. It had to stop!

Kendra knew her eyes were blazing as she flashed Ariane a furious look. "Ooohhhh!" Kendra growled from deep in her throat.

Ariane and Graham looked up and saw Kendra. Ariane blushed slightly and lowered her head.

Suddenly, there was a loud cracking noise at the window. Veins of light fractured the panes of glass. Then, with a violent explosion, the window burst apart. A storm of broken glass flew out into the room. One large, jagged piece sliced through the air, shining like a knife blade as it flew straight toward Ariane and Graham.

"No! Don't!" Kendra shrieked, horrified. She covered her eyes.

"What is it, Kendra?" Graham cried, startled.

Kendra dropped her hands from her face. She saw Graham looking around the room. Ariane sat with a stunned expression on her face. Her eyes were wide with terror.

Kendra gasped in shock.

"Kendra, what's the matter?" Graham asked. "Are you all right?"

Kendra pointed to the window. Graham turned to look at where she was pointing.

The window was whole again.

Graham looked baffled. "What's wrong?"

Kendra backed away. This was too bizarre. Ariane was looking at Kendra with a frightened expression. Had she seen the window shatter and that murderous piece of glass sail toward her? Did she know what Kendra was capable of?

All Kendra knew was that she was not imagining things. The window had smashed. And now the glass was unshattered. She had made it happen. She had put Ariane and Graham in mortal danger. And—somehow—she had stopped everything before it was too late.

Kendra was almost choking with horror as she raced up the stairs to her room. Revell was right. She did possess powers—terrible powers over which she had no control. How was she ever going to learn to live with them? And how was she going to stop herself from harming the person who seemed to bring her powers out in the worst possible way?

Kendra threw herself on her bed. Through her tears she wondered, How long can I control my anger toward Ariane?

CHAPTER 9

A little while later, as Kendra lay on her bed with tears in her eyes, a light knock sounded on her door.

"Kendra? It's Ariane. May I come in?"

"Go away."

"I have to speak to you. Please! It's very important!"

"No! Just leave me alone."

"Oh, please! I must talk to you. I want to explain. Let me come in—only for a moment."

Kendra felt her will weakening.

"Won't you open the door?" Ariane's soft voice pleaded from outside. "Please?"

Groaning, Kendra wiped her eyes and stood up. She crossed the room and opened the door a crack.

"Well?"

"May I come in?" Ariane asked.

"If you have to." She held the door open.

Ariane entered and sat on the edge of Kendra's desk chair.

Kendra looked at Ariane's wrist. It was bare.

Kendra dropped down in the big overstuffed armchair across from Ariane. She put her legs up on the footrest, waiting for Ariane's feeble explanation. She hoped she looked calmer than she felt.

"I—I shouldn't have," Ariane said. "I know it was wrong, but I couldn't help it." She held out her hand. Shining in her open palm was the gold-and-garnet bracelet.

Kendra looked at it, then looked away.

Ariane put the bracelet down on the desk.

"Thanks," Kendra said sharply. "It's always nice to get your property back."

"It isn't what you think. I wasn't going to steal it. I only wanted to borrow it—to show Uncle Graham. You see, he gave me the same bracelet years ago. There were two of them. Family—what do you call them?—heirlooms. He gave one to my cousin Syrie and the other to me. I felt so proud that he was treating me like his own daughter." Ariane's shoulders sagged, and she sat back in the chair. "I lost mine! I was so miserable, I cried for days."

Kendra shifted uncomfortably in the armchair. "That's still no excuse to steal my bracelet. I was going crazy looking for it. It means a lot to me."

"I knew I could never find another one like it," Ariane continued. "Then I saw the one you had. You never wore it, so I thought you wouldn't miss it for a while. I borrowed your bracelet so I could make Uncle Graham think I still had mine. I'm so grateful that he invited me here, and I only wanted to please him. I meant to put it back before you noticed it was gone. Please, I'm so s-sorry. I ask you to forgive me."

"When did you see my bracelet?" Kendra asked. "How did you know I had it?"

"Oh! I th-think—yes, it was when I borrowed your science notes. I noticed the jewelry box—"

"My notebook was on top of the dresser. My jewelry box was inside a drawer."

Ariane hung her head in shame. Tears rolled down her face.

"You were snooping through my things when I was out," Kendra accused her. "Even after I asked you not to. Do I have to put a lock on my door to keep you out?"

"N-no, I swear I'll never touch anything of yours again, Kendra. I was curious. I wanted to know everything about you. You are so American, so chic, and—what do you say?—cool. I was hoping to copy your style. So I couldn't help taking a small peek at your things. I wanted to be more like you. I thought maybe you and your friends would like me better."

"You've got to be kidding! Everyone practically rolls over and barks for you, Ariane. You couldn't be more popular."

"Not with everyone. Your friend Hallie doesn't seem to like me."

"Never mind her. I'm the one you have to get along with. And that'll never happen if I can't trust you."

"You can! Oh, I promise. Please, Kendra, can't we forget this ever happened and just be friends? That's all I want."

For the second time, Kendra was forced to accept Ariane's tearful apologies and assurances. She didn't see what other choice she had. Ariane would be living with her family for a whole year. Kendra couldn't keep giving Ariane the silent treatment forever. Besides, Kendra was still freaked out by the scene in the living room and how close she'd come to harming Ariane. She hoped Ariane would leave her things alone from now on.

After Ariane left, Kendra sat for a while. Then she picked up the bracelet and held it close. She was relieved to have this part of Syrie back. Kendra put the bracelet in the pocket of her old ski jacket—the one that held Michel's last letter. At least that was still there.

For the next few hours, Kendra buried herself in her Latin and calculus homework.

After dinner, she rummaged through her closet, hating everything on the hangers. She was going to Feathers tonight with her friends, even if she wasn't in the mood to party. She wasn't sure what she was in the mood for. The episode with Ariane and the window shattering had frightened her badly, so she didn't want to spend the evening alone, either.

And the memory of seeing Graham and Ariane together was haunting her. Had Ariane been telling the truth about the bracelet?

The outfit Kendra finally chose matched her feelings. She put on her most boring black dress and pulled her long hair back into a tight bun. She felt miserable, and she didn't want anyone complimenting her.

Nobody did.

Neil and the others took one look at her scowling face and gave her lots of room. For most of the night she stood against the wall, turning down every invitation to get out on the dance floor.

Kendra kept wondering why Ariane would take her bracelet. She didn't believe Ariane's feeble excuse.

I hate to mistrust Ariane, Kendra thought, but she gives me every reason to do so. Why do I feel this way?

Finally, Hallie approached her. "If you see Kendra," she whispered, "tell her she's missing a really cool scene."

In spite of herself, Kendra smiled and gave her friend a hug.

"I know," she replied. "I just can't make myself party tonight. I've got so much on my mind my head is spinning."

"I won't ask unless you feel like talking," Hallie promised.

"Thanks." Kendra nodded. "I don't want to talk about it, now. Go on and have fun. There's a cute guy over there, and he's looking right at you."

Hallie turned. "Hey, he is cute. See you later, Ken." Hallie weaved her way across the dance floor and was swallowed by the crowd.

Kendra's evening was a total disaster, and that's just what she was in the mood for.

CHAPTER 10

Kendra was asleep, dreaming about Revell. In her dream, she felt his hand brushing her hair from her cheek and his lips softly touching hers. The eerie music of the chimes floated on the air.

Then came the low, intimate voice from the shadows of her bedroom.

"Kendra. Wake up."

Kendra sat up groggily. Her room was pitch-black. She could barely make out the pile of clothing she had dropped when she came home from Feathers a couple of hours ago.

She rubbed her eyes and focused into the dark.

"Revell?" she whispered.

"I'm here," he answered in a hushed tone. "Are you ready, Kendra? Will you give me your promise? Say you will come with me. Say it now."

At the sound of his voice, the deep longing rippled through her. Revell had returned. He had come back to her. "I can't see you," she whispered back.

"You can hear me. You know what I want. Do you give me your promise?"

"Let me see you," she pleaded.

A wisp of light formed in the corner of the bedroom, then vanished. "No, Kendra. There's time enough for that—an eternity of time. Will you come with me now?"

Kendra shook her head, tears forming in her eyes. Being with Revell was something she wanted desperately. He was the only one who understood what she had been going through. But how could she go with him? To some world she didn't know? She was afraid of her powers and afraid of what would happen if she agreed to join him.

"I can't, Revell," she said. "I have to stay here."

"You can't deny your powers, Kendra," he warned her. "They're yours, whether you want them or not. You must learn to use them, to control them."

She shut her eyes. "I'll never use those powers again. They're dangerous, and they scare me." The scene in the living room replayed itself in her mind—the sound of the window exploding and glass slicing through the air toward Ariane. "Why did you ever tell me about them, Revell?"

A great sigh escaped from the dark corner as Revell's voice faded.

"You'll see, my love. I can wait."

As he faded away, Kendra buried her face in her pillow to muffle her agonized sobs. She had let him go. Would he ever return?

✦ ✦ ✦

On Saturday, Kendra and Hallie spent the afternoon shopping. They were looking for new shoes, but they had managed to case half the small boutiques on Madison Avenue. It was hard work, and they were hungry.

"What do you say—O'John's? I love their burgers." Hallie nudged Kendra toward the popular coffee shop a few doors away. It was still warm enough to sit outside at the tiny tables on the sidewalk, and they were lucky to find one free.

As they sipped their iced tea and waited for their burgers, Hallie eyed Kendra warily. "Want to talk?" she asked. "You were in a pretty bad mood last night at Feathers."

"Yeah, I know. Sorry."

Hallie shook her head. "What's the matter? Is it about Ariane again?"

"I guess." Kendra shrugged. "I just don't know what to think anymore. One minute she seems so sincere, and then, the next minute, I feel as though I shouldn't trust her. It's like a roller-coaster ride."

"What happened yesterday?" Hallie pressed her.

"When I walked in the door, Graham was looking at my bracelet on her wrist. You know it's been missing for weeks. Now suddenly it shows up on Ariane's arm." Her anger flared again. "She told me she was only borrowing it—which is fine if

I could really believe that—but why take it without asking me? I just don't get it."

"What did Graham say?" Hallie asked.

"Graham thinks the sun rises and sets on Ariane," Kendra said bitterly. "I can't complain to him."

"Why don't you pay Ariane back by taking her stuff? You know, make the punishment fit the crime?" Hallie suggested.

"Hallie, I'm shocked!" Kendra looked at her friend and pretended to look horrified. "What a mean, nasty, irresponsible idea! I love it!" Kendra laughed. "Maybe I will," she said.

But she knew she'd never snoop around Ariane's room again. Not after what happened last time. She couldn't trust herself or her powers.

The waitress came with their burgers and fries and set them down on the table. O'John's was a popular hangout for the students at Wilbraham. Kendra looked around inside the small restaurant, thinking she might see some of their friends. Instead, she saw something she didn't like. Sitting at one of the inside tables were Anthony and Ariane. They were smiling at each other and holding hands across the table. They seemed to be ignoring everyone around them, even though there were quite a few other Wilbraham students nearby.

Kendra turned back to look at Hallie, hoping her friend hadn't seen them too.

But Hallie had. Disappointment showed all

over her face. "Ah, love and lunch! How touching!" she remarked sarcastically.

Kendra squeezed her friend's hand sympathetically. "Come on, let's eat up and get out of here," she said.

They finished their burgers quickly, paid the bill, and left without looking in Anthony and Ariane's direction.

"I don't want them to see us," Hallie said, her voice shaking.

Kendra could see the pain in her friend's eyes. She wanted to comfort Hallie, but she was too angry. It was one thing for Ariane to steal Kendra's things, but seeing Hallie get hurt was a lot worse.

"Want to check out Willibald's?" Kendra asked, trying to be casual. "Their shoes are to die for, and it's right across the street."

"Sure, why not?" Hallie said without enthusiasm.

They crossed Madison and stood in front of the exotic display in the store window.

"Look at that," Hallie said, pointing.

It took Kendra only a second to realize that Hallie wasn't pointing at shoes, but at a reflection in the glass.

Across the street, Anthony and Ariane were just coming out of O'John's. They were still holding hands as they walked away from the restaurant. A coy smile played across Ariane's lips.

"Don't turn around," Kendra instructed, her voice tight with fury.

Hallie started to say something, but was cut off by the sudden sound of screaming in the street. Loud shrieks of warning filled the air.

The girls whirled around in panic.

Across the street, people were pointing frantically, screaming wildly. A few of them had even covered their eyes in horror.

Kendra saw what was happening as if it were in slow motion.

A battered yellow taxicab had jumped the curb. It was barreling out of control up the sidewalk toward Anthony and Ariane. In another instant, the two of them would be crushed.

"Oh no!" Kendra shrieked. Her heart leaped into her throat as she realized that Anthony and Ariane were going to be killed.

CHAPTER 11

The screams of the people in the street were deafening.

Kendra could feel a mighty force growing inside her body. The shouts around her faded as her concentration built. With a wild cry, she sent the total strength of her power at the yellow taxi as it hurtled up the sidewalk. "No! Don't!" she cried. "Do-o-o-on't!"

The taxi's brakes squealed. Its wheels locked. It skidded a few feet, then flipped over on its side. Metal scraped the pavement with a hideous screech. Glass flew everywhere, and steam from the taxi's radiator hissed and coiled up into the air.

The taxi had stopped only inches away from Anthony and Ariane.

Kendra and Hallie dashed across the street. Ariane had buried her face against Anthony's chest. She was sobbing quietly. Anthony was pale with shock as he held her.

"Oh, Anthony, I'm so glad you're okay!" Hallie cried.

Kendra stared at the battered taxi, stunned. Was it she who had caused it to stop like that? Had she really saved Anthony and Ariane?

Suddenly, another thought sliced through Kendra like a knife. She remembered her terrible anger at Ariane. Did she make this happen in the first place? Did she cause the taxi to lose control? She was sick with fear. Did she really have the powers Revell said? Had she used them to attack Ariane—risking Anthony's life, too?

Anthony's shaky voice snapped Kendra out of her thoughts. "He missed us only by a couple of inches."

"But you're okay," Hallie repeated. She touched Anthony lightly on the arm to reassure herself that he was unharmed.

In the distance a siren began to wail. A crowd gathered around the taxi. Through the shattered windshield, Kendra could see the driver struggling to free himself. Several people reached in to help him climb out.

Thank goodness the driver is okay too, Kendra thought. She shuddered and took a deep breath. What would have happened if she hadn't stopped the cab? The thought was unbearable.

In her heart, Kendra knew the truth. She had to face it. She did have powers, some sort of special gift that allowed her to make certain things happen at her will. And, luckily, she had just been able to use them to save lives.

But you've also caused destruction, a voice inside her warned. You must be very careful from now on!

Kendra's hands began to tremble, and she felt the blood drain out of her face.

"Ken, are you okay?" Hallie asked, concerned.

Kendra stared at Hallie, unable to speak. No, I'm not okay, she thought.

The fact was, she'd never be okay. Revell had warned her that she would use her powers again, but she had refused to believe him. Now she could see that everyone she cared about, everyone around her, was in danger. Terrible danger.

✦ ✦ ✦

Kendra didn't bother to undress for bed that night. She had no intention of sleeping. She was waiting for Revell. She had to see him. There must be some bargain she could make with him that would protect her friends and everyone she cared about. Maybe Revell could help her protect them. If he really loved her and wanted her to be strong, wouldn't he help her control her powers? She turned off the lights and sat in the chair at her desk. She listened for the chimes to start singing. She peered into the darkest corner of her room, hoping to see the firefly lights dancing. He would come to her. She was certain of it.

As she waited, she thought of her last meeting

with Revell. A faint smile came to her lips. She could almost see Revell's golden hair shining through the dark. She remembered the golden sparks that flashed in his piercing blue eyes when he bent his face close to hers. She could feel the electricity ripple through her body when he touched her. How she longed to feel the thrill of his kisses again!

At last, Kendra heard the soft tinkling of the chimes. She jumped to her feet.

"Revell!"

"I'm here, Kendra."

She glanced around her room, puzzled. Where was he? There were no lights and no movement in her room—just Revell's soft, seductive voice floating over the chimes. But the familiar warmth of pleasure rushed through her. She felt he was close.

"I've been watching you," Revell said. "I heard my name in your thoughts. Why did you call to me?"

"I can't see you," she said, puzzled.

"But you can hear me."

"Yes. Please, let me see you," she begged. Her entire being yearned for the sight of him.

He laughed softly. "Have you missed me?"

"Yes. Very much. Where are you?"

"Concentrate," he told her.

Kendra closed her eyes. A sudden vision of dark trees and bushes, long, dark mounds of earth, and white and rose-colored tombstones sprang to mind.

"The cemetery," she said aloud. "You're in the cemetery."

"That's right, my love." Revell sounded pleased. "If you want to see me . . . ."

His voice faded away. The air in her room grew cold and still, and she knew he was gone.

Longing and disappointment swept through her.

But she knew where to find him. This time he wanted her to come to him.

Quickly she headed down the stairs and into the dark night.

✦ ✦ ✦

Overhead the silvery full moon was high in the sky. Mist rose from the lawn as Kendra hurried to the cemetery. The closer she got, the higher the fog swirled around her, wrapping itself about her ankles and her knees like a living thing.

When she reached the graveyard, a sudden sound stopped her.

A high, plaintive cry trembled in the air.

"Kendra-a-a-a-a!"

Was someone hurt? Calling for help?

She stood, listening intently. Again, she heard the cry. It was loud and piteously mournful. This time, she knew what it was.

Syrie. She's calling to me.

Kendra hurried forward, moving through the smoky mist with cold fear gripping her whole body.

A vibrating light was hovering around Syrie's tombstone. Kendra slowed down, moving cautiously until she reached the edge of the cemetery. Yes, it was Syrie's grave shining faintly in the dark.

Suddenly, a dark shape moved in front of the light, partly blocking its glow. Kendra could see what the shape was. Someone was standing beside Syrie's grave, swaying slightly in the dark. A woman.

The figure turned slightly. She wasn't alone. A man was with her. They were wrapped in one another's arms, kissing passionately.

Kendra froze. She pressed herself against the trunk of a tree, hoping to get away without being seen.

A shaft of moonlight suddenly pierced the dark cover of leaves, falling on the woman's face.

It was Ariane!

The glow of the moon on Ariane's face spilled over and illuminated the man in her arms.

Kendra's stomach lurched when she saw who it was. Pain as sharp as a knife sliced through her heart.

Revell.

CHAPTER 12

Kendra gasped. Revell and Ariane! He was holding her, kissing her. His strong arms embraced Ariane the same way he had held Kendra. Ariane was clinging to him, returning his passionate kisses, just as Kendra had.

How could he?

Kendra was shocked. All her uneasiness and suspicions about Ariane must be true! Revell and Ariane knew each other—worse than that, they loved each other! And all this time, Kendra thought that Revell loved only her. Ariane had stolen him from her. Is that why she had come to live in Graham's home?

As Kendra stared at the lovers, the pain of her jealousy was unbearable.

She backed closer to the tree, making the dry leaves at her feet rustle. The noise startled the couple. They pulled apart and looked around.

Kendra blinked and goggled at them. Was she seeing things? That wasn't Revell with Ariane! It was Anthony!

But I just saw . . . .

A chilly breeze stirred through the trees. The crystal chimes began to sing. Revell's soft laughter suddenly rose in the night air.

Kendra stood frozen against the tree. How could Revell laugh at her? Was he deliberately teasing her to make her jealous? How could he be so cruel? I have to get out of here! she thought.

She moved, and the leaves at her feet rustled again.

Ariane broke away from Anthony. "Who's that?" she called. She stepped cautiously toward the tree where Kendra stood. "What are you doing here?" Ariane demanded harshly.

Anthony came up behind her. Even the darkness couldn't hide the embarrassment on his face.

"Hey, Ken," he said. "Out for a late evening stroll?"

"She's spying on me, that's what she's doing," Ariane snarled. "Isn't that right, Kendra? You followed us, just so you could check up on me."

"N-no, I wasn't. I just didn't know—uh, who was here."

"Who did you think it was?" For a moment, Ariane sounded so smug that Kendra wondered if she knew what Kendra had just seen—Ariane with Revell, not Anthony. Ariane's eyes were blazing as she continued her attack. "You are so sure you know all about me, aren't you? You just keep spying on me to prove you're right."

"Ariane," Anthony said, trying to calm her. "I'm sure Kendra would never—"

But Ariane wasn't listening.

"What right do you have to follow me? This afternoon at O'John's you came out of nowhere— and now you're here. I won't have you spying on me, Kendra! I'll tell Uncle Graham."

As Ariane raved, her voice grew louder and more shrill. But before Kendra had a chance to say anything else, a huge, dark shape dashed into the cemetery. Kendra stiffened, then relaxed as she realized it was Max. But why did he look so wild?

Max's deep-throated bark split the night. He bared his fangs and rushed at Ariane.

"Max! No!" Anthony yelled.

Max wheeled around for a second and growled at Anthony.

Kendra was shocked. She had never seen the usually sweet dog turn on his master like that. But it was Ariane he was really after.

He turned back to Ariane, barking fiercely. Then he leaped at the terrified girl. With a shake of his heavy head, he sank his teeth into Ariane's leg.

"No!" Anthony shouted. "Stop, Max!" Anthony made a frantic dive, but he couldn't catch the dog.

Ariane screamed at Max in French and tried to kick him. He backed away out of her reach, growling. Then he began barking again as he prepared to jump at her in another attack.

"Down, Max!" Kendra screamed. "Don't!"

Max hesitated, then flopped heavily to the ground. He looked over at Kendra and whined.

Ariane swung her leg again to kick him, but he twisted away from her foot and escaped to Kendra's side.

"What's gotten into you?" Anthony yelled and grabbed for his collar. But Max was too fast. He slipped away from Anthony's grasp and raced out of the cemetery.

Everything had happened in a flash. They all stared after the dog, too stunned for a moment to speak.

Surprisingly, Max's bite had barely broken the skin. They led Ariane back to the house, and Kendra left Anthony to patch Ariane up with antiseptic and a Band-Aid.

Max had disappeared, but Kendra was too exhausted to search for him. Instead, she undressed quickly and climbed into bed. She couldn't stop thinking about all the strange events of the day— seeing Ariane and Anthony together at O'John's; the taxi losing control and nearly running them down; Revell and Ariane kissing—and Revell suddenly changing into Anthony. And now Max's odd behavior toward Ariane.

Why did the dog dislike Ariane so much? Kendra knew that dogs often had a sixth sense about people. Maybe the Labrador retriever sensed something suspicious about Ariane, just as Kendra did.

She sighed and fluffed her pillow, eager to get

some sleep. But when she closed her eyes, all she could think about was the couple embracing in the cemetery. She had seen Revell kissing Ariane. She knew she had. How could he have lured Kendra to the graveyard just to laugh at her that way?

Then another thought struck her. Maybe he was involved in everything that had happened today. Why was he trying to torment her like this?

She rolled over and forced herself to think about something else—next week's calculus assignment. But thoughts of Revell would not go away. He had said he loved her. She could feel his love whenever they were together. Why was she so overcome with doubts and suspicions? Revell wouldn't deliberately be cruel to her. He wouldn't harm someone she loved, like Anthony.

Then she remembered Neil's fall over the cliff, and the window glass flying at Graham.

No, Revell wouldn't do such terrible things on purpose, she protested.

Or would he?

✦ ✦ ✦

Shortly before dawn, Kendra was awakened.

The house was quiet. What had roused her? Her door was partly open. She listened intently.

There it was! That sound.

The noise outside her room was a terrible, rasping breathing. Someone was coming up the stairs to the third floor. Slowly, heavily, climbing as if each step was agony.

Thump-flop . . . thump-flop . . . thump-flop . . . .

Kendra shrunk back against the pillows, shaking. The sound grew louder. It was coming closer.

Thump-flop . . . thump-flop . . . thump . . .

The door to her room was slowly pushed open.

She gasped—then sighed with relief when she saw it was Max.

"Well, you sure did scare me, big fellow!"

She watched him lumber into the room. As he came toward her bed, Kendra saw he was staggering. His breathing was a horrible croak. Without warning, he collapsed on the floor, panting and wheezing. He couldn't even lift his head.

Kendra was horrified. She leaped out of bed and knelt at the dog's side.

"Max! What is it? What's wrong?" She gathered him in her arms and stroked his trembling body.

He looked up at her. His eyes were bloodshot and yellow. For an instant, they stared up at Kendra, pleading. Then they rolled back in his head. A gurgling rattle came from deep in his throat. Thick, white foam bubbled at the corners of his mouth.

"Oh, Max! What happened?" Kendra cried.

Suddenly, Max shivered in a violent convulsion.

A sob rose in Kendra's throat. The big black Lab was dying!

CHAPTER 13

Kendra ran to the top of the stairs, calling frantically. "Anthony! Graham! Help!"

She flew down the steps, shouting at the top of her lungs.

The whole house woke in shock. Graham was the first out of his room, tugging on his robe. Dinah peered out of the door behind him. Anthony rushed into the hall in his rumpled pajamas, and Mrs. Stavros appeared at the top of the first-floor stairs, bundled up in a heavy woolen bathrobe.

"It's Max! He's sick! I think he's dying!" Kendra cried. She dashed back up the steps, followed closely by Graham and Anthony.

Ariane stood outside Kendra's room, peering anxiously inside. "What's the matter?" she asked in a timid voice. "Is Max okay?"

Kendra brushed past her, too worried to bother explaining.

Graham and Anthony rushed inside and knelt

over Max, who was heaving and choking on the floor. Together, they carried the big dog carefully down the stairs and laid him on the sofa in the living room. While Dinah phoned for a car to take Max to the animal hospital, the men hastily threw on some clothes.

When the car arrived a few minutes later, Anthony and Graham carried Max outside. They placed him gently in the back seat and drove away.

For Kendra, the waiting was agony. She sat in grim silence at the kitchen table with Ariane, Dinah, and Mrs. Stavros, who had made tea and hot chocolate. Finally, Dinah stood up and announced that she was going back to bed. Mrs. Stavros was the next to give up the vigil. She asked Kendra to let her know about Max when Anthony and Graham returned.

That left Kendra and Ariane facing each other across the table. After a few uncomfortable moments of not speaking or looking at each other, Ariane rose and tightened the belt of her pink satin robe.

"I guess there isn't anything I can do. I'm going back to bed now. I hope your dog is all right."

What a phony! Kendra couldn't help thinking as she watched Ariane leave. The French girl didn't look upset at all. If anything, she looked relieved, almost satisfied. Kendra remembered how Ariane had tried to kick Max earlier. After

Max's attack, Kendra couldn't exactly blame her for not shedding tears over the dog. But, somehow, Kendra blamed her for the change in Max. Before Ariane came to live with them, Max had been a sweet, predictable, and loyal dog. But, ever since her arrival, his behavior was so odd Kendra scarcely recognized him at times.

Kendra was miserable as the hours ticked by, but she couldn't bear the thought of going back upstairs until she knew how Max was.

At last, Graham and Anthony returned. They looked exhausted. Their faces immediately told Kendra the news wasn't good.

"Max is still alive, but the vet isn't sure what's wrong with him," Anthony said flatly. "It looks like he may have been poisoned, but the vet's not certain."

"Poisoned?" Kendra could feel her mouth drop open. "How could he have been poisoned?"

Anthony shrugged. "Who knows. Maybe he ate something he shouldn't have. At any rate, the vet doesn't expect him to survive—and that might be the best thing. Max was suffering terribly, even though the vet was doing everything possible to help him."

Kendra climbed the stairs to her room, tears in her eyes. How could Max swallow something so dangerous it could kill him? He was too smart for that. Had someone fed him the poison? Why would anyone do such a horrible thing? And who?

She brushed the tears from her cheeks, remembering how Max had sought her out when he got sick. Why didn't he go to Graham or Anthony? What had made the suffering animal come to her when his masters were closer? Max had climbed all the way up to the third floor to find Kendra—in agony the whole way. It didn't make sense.

✦ ✦ ✦

Kendra sank into bed and slept heavily until early afternoon. It was a gloomy Sunday. The sky was cloudy, matching her mood perfectly. She tugged on a pair of jeans and went down for something to eat.

Anthony was just leaving the table. He told her that Max was still hanging on and Graham had gone to see him.

Anthony looked miserable. Kendra knew he felt just as bad—or worse—than she did. She put her arm around him and hugged him quickly. "Maybe Max will pull through," she said.

"I hope so." Anthony managed a weak smile, then headed for his room.

Kendra ate a quick bite, then went up to her room to study. She didn't even bother to call Hallie or any of her friends. She didn't feel like talking to anyone today.

Later, Kendra wandered back downstairs to look out the front door. If it wasn't too cold and if it hadn't started raining yet, maybe she'd go for a walk.

Passing through the hall, she saw an unopened letter lying on the table next to the door. It was from Lauren, and it was addressed to her. She'd been so busy yesterday, she hadn't even checked the mail.

Kendra stuffed the letter into the pocket of her heavy Irish knit sweater and decided to take her walk. She left the house and headed for the cemetery. It would be quiet and private there.

She settled cross-legged on the stone bench near Syrie's and Helen's graves and pulled out Lauren's letter.

She began reading.

> "Hey, Kennie. . . . Did you forget me? You haven't written in weeks—okay, two weeks. I keep checking for a letter, but it feels like ages since I heard from you. So who's the new guy in your life that's keeping you so busy? I mean, it's got to be somebody special or else no excuse!"

Kendra smiled. Her most recent letter was probably in Lauren's hands by now. Suddenly she missed her sister terribly. Somehow, if Lauren were here, things would be a lot better.

She continued reading the long, gossipy letter to the end, missing Lauren more with each page.

> "So write right away and tell me what's happening at Wilbraham. I miss you lots. Love, love, love! P.S. Don't forget, a hug and a Twinkie for Vinnie!

P.P.S. A hug and a scratch behind the
ears for Max!"

When Kendra read the dog's name, her joy
evaporated. How was she ever going to tell Lauren
about Max's being sick? Poor Lauren! She'd be
heartbroken. Her sister had a special bond with
the dog that had grown very strong in the short
time they had been living in the old mansion.

Kendra folded the letter and tucked it back in
her pocket. With a deep sigh, she looked out
across the green lawn.

"Oh, no!" she groaned softly. She was about to
have company.

The figure heading across the grass toward her
was Ariane. She looked upset.

Okay, what is it this time? Kendra thought as
Ariane came up to her. It couldn't be more bad
news about Max; Ariane wouldn't look that upset.

Ariane stood hesitantly for a moment, then took
a deep breath.

"I'm really sorry about last night, Kendra," she
began. "About what happened in the cemetery. I
didn't mean to yell at you like that." Her face
flushed as she continued. "I couldn't sleep, so I
thought I would go visit Aunt Helen's grave—and
Syrie's. I hoped it would calm me. You see, I really
loved them both, very much. I was always so
happy when they came to visit us in Paris. Cousin
Syrie especially." She looked down at Syrie's
tombstone. Tears clouded her eyes, and her voice

dropped sadly. "I was sick for weeks when I learned that she was dead."

Kendra glanced at Ariane quickly. What was she saying? How well could she have known her cousin Syrie when they lived an ocean apart? How often had they seen each other? Ariane was telling her that she felt close to Syrie. Was Ariane a Sensitive, too? Did she share the same bond that Kendra felt for the dead girl?

Kendra searched Ariane's face for an answer, but there was no clue on her smooth features. The tears were in her eyes, the sadness was in her voice, but otherwise Ariane seemed calm and unaffected by what she was saying.

Ariane continued. "I was coming down the stairs last night when Anthony heard me. He said he'd come with me. We went together, and—well, what happened, happened. It's not a secret that he likes me, that we like each other."

Like? Kendra thought. Haven't you noticed he's bonkers over you?

"And when I saw you under the tree, watching us, I thought you had followed us. It looked like you were spying on me. I got angry." Her voice broke. "I didn't mean to kick Max or hurt him in any way. But he attacked me."

"He was just trying to protect me," Kendra said bitterly. "I've never seen him act like that, but you were screaming, and I guess he thought you were going to attack me." She looked Ariane in the eyes.

The tears had disappeared as quickly as they had come. "Why would you think I'd spy on you? I don't care what you and Anthony do."

Ariane shrugged. "You always seem to be around whenever I'm doing something—personal."

"You mean, like, at O'John's? Get real, will you? Everyone from Wilbraham goes there. Besides, since when did lunch become something 'personal'?"

"Well, then, that time in the kitchen. You were spying on me and Mrs. Stavros."

"Oh, please! I went into my kitchen in my house, and the two of you acted like I was breaking and entering!"

"I was trying to keep it a secret, but I may as well tell you now. I knew that Uncle Graham's birthday was coming up. I wanted to arrange a surprise for him. So I was telling Mrs. Stavros about a special dish my mother always makes for him when he comes to Paris—a wonderful coq au vin. He loves it. I thought he'd be really pleased if we made it for his birthday."

"You mean all that whispering with Mrs. Stavros, that big conspiracy of yours, was about a dumb chicken casserole? I don't believe it!"

"Honestly, Kendra," Ariane went on, "I'm just trying to fit in here. I want Uncle Graham to be glad he invited me to come. Anthony, too. And especially you. But everything I do makes you angry. I don't know why you dislike me so much!"

Oh, boy, here come the tears again, Kendra thought.

"I don't dislike you, Ariane. You just make me—nervous or something. I mean, my stuff disappears, and then it turns up in your room or on your wrist."

"I b-bet you think I did something to Max, too!" Ariane said, sniffling. "I told you, I'd never do anything to hurt him."

Kendra didn't respond. Instead she stared at the other girl. She didn't know what to make of Ariane, and right now she didn't have the energy to try to figure it out.

"Please, believe me. I just want us to be friends," Ariane said in a small, sad voice.

Kendra reached into her pocket and handed Ariane a small package of Kleenex. She sighed heavily. "Okay, Ariane, I believe you. Let's try again. We can be friends as long as you leave my things alone—and you try to think twice before jumping to conclusions about me and what I'm doing."

Ariane smiled at her through her tears. "I will. I promise."

Kendra tried to smile back.

✦ ✦ ✦

After Ariane left, Kendra sat on the bench for a few more minutes. Then she got up, planning to return to her room and answer Lauren's letter right away. She wouldn't mention Max yet, she decided. Maybe by the end of the week they'd have better news to report.

As she turned to leave the cemetery, Kendra glanced toward the spot where she had seen Ariane and Anthony—or Ariane and Revell—locked in an embrace. A terrible pang of jealousy sliced through Kendra. The memory of Revell with someone else was almost too much for her to bear.

Desire for him washed over her. When would she see him again? How she longed to feel his caress, to feel his sweet, soft lips on hers.

Suddenly, a mournful cry filled the air. Uneasily, Kendra glanced toward the grave where Syrie was buried. The sound was coming from that direction.

The moaning rose, louder. It was an eerie, ominous cry that pierced the air like a siren. Then, as abruptly as it had begun, the moaning stopped.

Kendra shivered. Was that Syrie, trying to send her some kind of message about Revell? About Ariane?

Why would I think that? she wondered. Quickly, Kendra shook off the thought and hurried back toward the house. I'm really starting to lose it.

CHAPTER 14

"Hallie! Guess what!" Kendra said excitedly into the phone.

"You've been signed by CBS to be their news anchor? No? Okay, you're eloping to Hawaii with Rob Prentis, King of the Dweebs? You're—"

"Goodbye, Hallie."

"No, wait! What's up?"

"If you can get serious for a minute, I'll tell you. Michel is coming to New York—Michel Lamont! I just got a letter from him from Paris. He'll be here in another week."

"How come?"

"He's between semesters in Paris. He got his folks to agree to let him spend a week here. Isn't that cool?"

"Is Jean-Louis coming, too?"

"Nope, just Michel."

"Oh, well," Hallie sighed. "I should have kept writing to Jean-Louis. But at least we'll see Michel again."

"Michel thinks he might like to go to college here in the States. Maybe even in New York," Kendra went on. "He wants to check out some schools."

"Where's he staying? With you?"

"No, with a friend in his dorm at Columbia University. That's one of the colleges he's interested in. He's thinking about journalism as a career, like me, and Columbia's got a great department. He'll only be here for a week, but he says he hopes we'll get to see a lot of each other."

"Won't Neil be thrilled," Hallie said. "That'll help you two get back together again."

"Neil will definitely not be thrilled," Kendra admitted. "But I'm not going to let that prevent me from hanging out with Michel. We should plan some fun things to do with him—show him the local scene."

"Hey, I'll be glad to cut classes and show him around," Hallie joked. "I think he's real cute. In fact, I remember when we met at the museum, I was the one he spoke to first. Poor guy—he's been suffering without me for all these months."

"You wish!"

"That's right," Hallie replied. "I do. Especially since I've had to totally give up on Anthony, with Ariane in the picture."

They stayed on the phone a little while longer, chatting about places they could take Michel while he was in town.

"How's Max?" Hallie asked before they hung up.

"Still hanging in there," Kendra told her.

"I'm so sorry, Ken."

"I know," Kendra said with a sigh. "But he's lasted this long. Maybe there's still room for hope. Talk to you later."

✦ ✦ ✦

Michel called Kendra as soon as he arrived in New York. She invited him over for dinner, but he said he was exhausted from his trip. They made a date for the following day.

When the doorbell rang at four o'clock the next afternoon, Kendra rushed downstairs to open the door. "Michel!" she cried. "It's great to see you again."

"*Bonjour,*" Michel replied. He kissed her on both cheeks in the typical French manner and held out an elegant bouquet of white tulips.

"They're beautiful! Thank you," she said, taking the freshly cut flowers from him. "Come on in and meet my family."

Inside the house, Kendra found a vase for the tulips, then brought Michel into the living room to meet Graham and Dinah.

Michel shook their hands and said to Graham, "What a beautiful house you have! So unusual. It must be quite old. Have you lived here long?"

Graham beamed with pleasure. He loved the old house on 76th Street and welcomed any opportunity to talk about it. He immediately whisked away Michel for a tour.

"What a lovely boy, Kendra!" Dinah told her as soon as Michel and Graham were out of earshot. "Such good manners."

Kendra smiled. Michel was polite—and very cute, too.

After Graham's house tour, Kendra found Michel a racket and led him outside to the tennis court. Hallie and Anthony were already there, playing singles.

Hallie greeted Michel, then introduced him to Anthony.

Anthony and Michel shook hands. "Nice to meet you," Anthony said. "Are you up for doubles?"

Michel nodded, gesturing to the racket he was carrying. "Kendra promised me I would have the chance to beat some Americans at tennis. I'm ready."

Anthony grinned. "We'll see about that."

The four of them played several sets before dinner.

For Kendra, the afternoon was really great. Michel had a cool sense of humor. She couldn't remember the last time she had felt so relaxed and happy. It had definitely been before Ariane's arrival.

After their game, Anthony loaned Michel some swimming trunks, and they all jumped into the pool to cool off. Then they dressed and trooped into the dining room for dinner.

Dinah and Graham were already seated. They were talking to Ariane, who had been out all afternoon. When Kendra walked in with Michel, Ariane nearly dropped the water glass she was holding.

"Oh, hello, Michel," she said, flustered.

Michel returned her greeting, then glanced away with an uncomfortable look on his face.

Anthony was surprised. "You two know each other?" he asked.

"We've met once or twice," Michel said. "Ariane is a friend of a friend."

Ariane nodded. She recovered her poise enough to exchange a few words with Michel in French. They spoke too quickly for Kendra to understand. But she could feel the tension between them.

Kendra shot another glance at Ariane. What's her story? And why does Michel seem so uneasy around her? Did it have to do with what Michel had written about Ariane? About the trouble she'd had in Paris?

Immediately after dinner, Ariane excused herself and went upstairs to her room. The others watched a movie on TV, then Hallie and Michel left. Kendra and Anthony walked out into the gardens for a short stroll.

"Do you know why Graham invited Ariane for such a long visit?" Kendra asked as they walked through the perfumed flower beds.

"No, but I'm sure glad he did. She's something special, isn't she?" He stopped suddenly, remembering how Ariane had exploded at Kendra in the cemetery. "I mean, even if she does have a temper."

"She's okay," Kendra said reluctantly. "But it seemed so sudden. I mean, she just showed up one day without any warning—and now she's a permanent new member of the family."

"Not so new. After all, she's known Graham all her life. You can see how attached they are to each other. Besides, she'll be going home at the end of the year." His voice drooped at the thought.

"I know. But didn't you wonder why he invited her in the first place?"

"Well, yeah, I did. I asked him, but he got really angry. He told me to mind my own business. He hasn't snapped at me like that in ages. I wasn't going to push him for an explanation."

"Didn't you think it was strange?"

Anthony turned to her. "What are you getting at?"

"I thought maybe you'd be curious enough to look into her background. You know, her past—her relationship with Graham."

"You mean, investigate my own father?" Anthony laughed, while Kendra looked away, embarrassed. "Well, maybe I should. I'll see what I can find out, okay?"

"Sure." Kendra sighed. Sometimes it seemed as

if she'd never get to the bottom of the mystery surrounding Ariane.

✦ ✦ ✦

For the rest of the weekend, Kendra spent nearly every waking moment with Michel. His friend at Columbia was busy studying for an exam, so Kendra and her friends showed him the city. They all had a great time.

They went to a jazz concert at Lincoln Center, to Tower Records, to a couple of movies and espresso bars on Third Avenue, to Feathers and Big Camille's, another hot downtown club, and to the Central Park Zoo, where Kendra and Anthony actually had to drag Michel away from the penguin house and the polar bears in the underwater tank. He loved animals and was very sympathetic when she told him about Max, who was still in the hospital.

Neil was with them most of the time. Kendra had gotten over being angry and had called him to make up. She might not be interested in him as a boyfriend—and she was honest with him about that—but she reminded him that they had been good friends for a long time. She didn't want a quarrel between them to last forever. He was glad to hear from her, even if he understood that it was friendship, not love, that had prompted her to call. He joined the group showing Michel the town. And he did a pretty good job of hiding his disappointment.

Once or twice Ariane came out with them and acted as a translator whenever Michel's English broke down. She and Michel seemed to have gotten over their initial uneasiness, but they weren't exactly friendly toward each other.

Politely distant is more like it, Kendra thought.

On Sunday evening, Anthony and Ariane decided to go out for dinner. Kendra stayed home with Dinah and Graham and invited Michel for dinner. Mrs. Stavros had promised to serve Michel a real American meal. She lived up to her promise by creating a feast of fried chicken, mashed potatoes with gravy, and freshly baked biscuits, all of which Michel enjoyed to the very last bite.

After dinner, Kendra took Michel for a walk along the high path overlooking the river. She was careful not to let either of them get too close to the edge of the cliff. She hadn't forgotten Neil's "accident." She wasn't going to risk anything like that happening again.

As they walked, Kendra kept sneaking looks at Michel. Throughout the weekend, she had found him more and more attractive. He wasn't as tall as Neil or Anthony, but he was very handsome in a different way. He was thin and had high cheekbones, straight, dark blond hair which he wore long, and warm brown eyes.

When Michel caught Kendra looking at him, he smiled at her without saying anything.

They continued to walk for a while in silence,

then stood looking out over the river at the lights rippling in the water.

"I must thank you for a wonderful weekend, Kendra. You were so good to show me around—you and your friends. I have had a most perfect time."

"It's been fun for us, too," she responded enthusiastically. "You've got a talent for getting along with everyone. It's awesome."

"Awesome," he repeated. "That's, like, cool, *n'est-ce pas?*"

"Yes," she agreed with a laugh. "It's awesome and cool the way everyone likes you." She paused. "Although Ariane isn't exactly your best friend, is she?"

At the mention of Ariane's name, Michel looked away and became silent again.

Kendra peered at him closely. "What is it about her, Michel? You mentioned something in one of your letters, some kind of trouble?"

He shook his head quickly. "No, it is nothing. Just rumors. I don't like to tell tales when I don't know really if they are true."

Kendra didn't want to press him, but she couldn't help herself.

"Was it something she did? In Paris? Something bad?"

"N-no, not exactly. It was more an accident, probably. A terrible tragedy."

"Please, Michel, tell me," she said softly. "I need to know."

He looked at her, puzzled, then shrugged. "Very well, but you understand I do not know anything personally—only the story that another student told me. I wouldn't like others to hear it."

"I understand."

"It happened last year," he said, looking down at the river. "Ariane was always very popular. She liked many boys, but not as many as all the ones who liked her. There was one boy she went out with a few times and then refused to see anymore. He was really in love with her—or he thought he was—and he wouldn't leave her alone. She tried to make him understand how she felt, but he wouldn't listen. Finally, Ariane was very cruel to him."

"What happened?" Kendra asked.

Michel glanced over at her. "They found him hanging from a light fixture. He was dead."

Kendra gasped.

"There was no note. There were rumors, stories. After an investigation, the police said his death was a suicide, but some people were not convinced." He shrugged. "I don't know. Maybe it was. But even when his friends and family tried to accept that it was suicide, Ariane still got blamed. My friend said she was so heartless toward the boy who died."

Kendra stared at Michel in horror. It was Ariane's fault that some boy had killed himself. Or worse, she had been suspected of being directly involved in his death—in his possible murder.

Michel turned to face her. "You can see why I would not want you to say anything to anyone else. Ariane was frightened when she saw me here. I think she is afraid that I will reveal her past. Please keep this story to yourself."

Kendra nodded. "I promise."

Michel smiled at her. "It is easy to trust you. You are a very honest person."

"I try," Kendra replied, smiling back.

Michel gazed at her with a thoughtful expression.

She nudged him gently. "What're you thinking about?"

Michel shrugged. "Tell me, do you think you can be so much in love that you would rather die than live without someone's love?"

Kendra thought for a moment, caught off guard by the seriousness of his question.

"I know it happens," she answered slowly. "But I'm not sure that's really love. I think it's more like a sickness, an obsession. You know, people become obsessed with someone and then think they can't live without them." She shuddered. "It seems dangerous to fall in love like that."

Michel was watching her face as she spoke. He reached out to touch her hair. "You are wonderful, Kendra," he said softly. "I could fall in love with you. Would you mind?"

She shook her head. "I don't think so."

He pulled her gently into his arms and kissed her. Kendra kissed him back.

Unexpectedly, the delicate sound of crystal chimes rang in her ears. An image of Revell flashed into her mind. All she could think of was Revell's strong arms, the soft touch of his hands, the way her lips responded to his kiss. She was filled with a burning desire for him.

The chimes sang out like a warning. A voice whispered in her ear: "Kendra. You belong to me. Remember that."

Kendra pulled away from Michel quickly.

He looked at her, his expression serious as he studied her face. "There is someone else? Is it Neil? I thought he was just a friend."

Kendra shook her head, more confused than ever. She had wanted Michel to kiss her, and she wanted to kiss him back. But now Revell had come between them.

She looked away, not knowing what to say. "Actually," she began, "there is someone else."

"I understand." Michel touched her face delicately. "I accept that. May we still be friends? Would you like that?"

"Yes," Kendra said. "Very much."

"Awesome," he replied, smiling at her.

Kendra forced herself to smile back at him, but her heart wasn't in it. After three days of fun, her good mood had been ruined.

CHAPTER 15

That night, Kendra lay awake, too confused to sleep. What did Revell really want from her? She had thought he loved her and wanted to help her develop her powers—but not to use them to attack people, like Anthony and Ariane. Not to kill!

Her thoughts tormented her as she tossed in bed. Finally, she turned on her light and picked up the romance novel lying in the stack on her night table. The only way to get through this night, she decided, was to read until her mind stopped churning. It took almost an hour before her book dropped from her hands and her eyes shut from pure exhaustion.

In the morning, Kendra pulled herself out of bed, feeling completely drained. It would be a busy day. She had a history quiz this morning, and she had arranged with Mr. Taylor to let Michel visit Wilbraham and observe the TV studio workshop. Also, she was scheduled to be on camera again this afternoon.

She checked her bathroom mirror and groaned when she saw her tired face and bloodshot eyes. She hopped into the shower, hoping the warm water would revive her spirits as well as her body.

✦ ✦ ✦

Before the TV workshop began, she met Michel outside the studio.

"I am so excited," he told her. "Hallie told me how wonderful you are on TV. Now I will see for myself."

Kendra smiled her thanks and led him inside. Neil and Ariane were already there. Both nodded coolly when Kendra and Michel entered. Obviously, neither one was very happy to see Michel. But Mr. Taylor greeted the French student warmly. He gave Michel a brief tour and told him the background of some of the technology used in the studio.

Michel became quickly absorbed in watching the preparations for the broadcast. He was eager to learn everything he could about the lights and cameras. While he was busy, Kendra decided to review her notes before appearing on camera. She sat quietly in a corner of the control booth, studying the pages.

A few minutes later, Mr. Taylor called to her from across the studio. When she looked up, he pointed to the clock on the wall. "Air time," he said.

Kendra stood up, smoothed her hair, and left the control booth to take her place on the set.

The bright spotlights flashed in her eyes as she settled herself at the desk to read the school news. Several students rolled the cameras toward her, and others scurried around to adjust the lighting.

"Ready, Kendra?" one of the camera people called.

She nodded confidently. She was eager to show off her skill in front of Michel. Being on-camera was something she loved, and she knew she was poised and professional. She could see Michel watching her from the corner of the control booth. He flashed her a grin and a thumbs-up.

Just before the cameras began to roll, Kendra noticed Ariane walk over to Michel. Ariane rested her hand on the tall metal stand of a huge, heavy spotlight that wasn't being used at the moment. She leaned over to whisper something in Michel's ear. He scowled at whatever she was saying and waved his hand as if to brush her off.

"Kendra!" Mr. Taylor called. "Stay alert. We're on in ten seconds."

Embarrassed, Kendra turned back to the cameras. She was furious at Ariane. Thanks to her, Kendra had become flustered and was off to a shaky start.

The cameras began to roll. Kendra started reading from the teleprompter scrolling above the camera. Suddenly, she noticed a movement in the back of the control booth. The spotlight that Ariane was touching began to topple. It was falling. It was going to crash right on top of Michel!

Kendra watched in horror as the huge metal light hit Michel's head and knocked him over. He fell against the corner of the control desk as the heavy light smashed onto the electronic panel. The lens of the spotlight shattered, sending thick splinters of glass flying. A shower of sparks sprayed into the air. With a loud crack, all the lights went out, plunging the entire studio into darkness.

Kendra jumped to her feet. Frantically, she tried to find her way off the set and back into the control booth. In the darkness, she couldn't see more than a foot in front of her. Around her, everyone was screaming.

As soon as she pushed open the soundproof door, she heard one especially high-pitched scream, louder than the rest. It was Michel. His body was outlined in sizzling blue light, dancing jerkily as an electric current coursed through him. His cry rose above the angry buzz of electricity and the other students' screams.

Kendra rushed toward Michel. She felt someone brush against her in the dark. She smelled a familiar perfume. Ariane.

Kendra remembered what she had seen just before the light fell. Ariane had been leaning over to talk to Michel, her hand holding onto the light stand. Had she deliberately pushed the spotlight over? Was she trying to kill Michel?

"What have you done now?" Kendra howled at Ariane. Nobody could have heard her over all the shrieking and the angry buzzing of the electricity. But she wouldn't have cared if anyone had. She turned to Michel. "No, no! Don't!" she screamed.

An instant later there was a loud thump. The lights in the studio came on suddenly.

Everyone stood frozen and silent for a second, staring. Then a hushed murmuring rose through the studio.

Michel was lying on the floor next to the console, not moving. His eyes were closed. Blood streamed down his face from a gash in his forehead where the spotlight had hit him.

Mr. Taylor and Kendra ran over to him. They both knelt at his side. Tears stung Kendra's eyes as she watched the instructor take Michel's wrist between his fingers. Then Mr. Taylor sighed and leaned back on his heels.

At that moment, Michel groaned and opened his eyes. He was alive.

"*Mon Dieu,*" he said, speaking French in his bewilderment. He looked up and saw Kendra, her face ghostly white, peering down at him. "Wh-what happened?"

"The spotlight fell over," Kendra told him. "It hit you and knocked you down."

Mr. Taylor helped Michel to his feet. "You also took a jolt of electricity when the control panel short-circuited. Are you all right?" He handed

Michel a handkerchief for the cut on his forehead, studying him with concern.

Michel nodded. He looked weak and shaken. "It's just this cut on my head, I think."

"Well, let's get you to the nurse," Mr. Taylor told him.

"I'm feeling fine now," Michel protested. "Just a little fall."

But Mr. Taylor was firm. "I insist on it. Come on, we'll get that cut fixed up and have you checked over, just to be certain."

Suddenly, tears welled up in Kendra's eyes. First Neil and now Michel. Who would be next? Was everyone around her in jeopardy?

"Oh, Michel," she cried, unable to stop herself. She threw her arms around him in a fierce hug. Then she backed off, embarrassed. She helped Mr. Taylor and Neil lead Michel out of the studio and down the hall to the school nurse's infirmary.

She was aware that Ariane was watching them go, her eyes cold and hard.

CHAPTER 16

Kendra quietly sobbed herself to sleep that night. Michel hadn't been hurt badly this time, but what would happen next time? She felt tormented by the danger that surrounded her. Danger that she was sure Ariane was responsible for. It seemed as though Ariane was trying to ruin her life. She had to convince someone—but how? No one would believe her.

Kendra fell asleep, tears of helplessness still wet on her cheeks.

◆ ◆ ◆

Hours later, Kendra awoke, feeling uneasy. In the dark, frightening thoughts whirled through her mind. She decided to take a walk around the grounds outside to clear her head.

As she headed around the side of the old mansion, she saw a dull light shining beyond the gardens. It came from the old shed—the one that Mr. Stavros, the housekeeper's husband, had told her was never used. It was always kept locked, he had said when she tried to enter it. She shivered, remembering how Mr. Stavros had tried to warn her away from the shed just before he died.

Kendra should stay away. She knew it. Still, something compelled her to investigate the mysterious light.

She heard voices coming from inside the shed as she came closer.

"Why would you want to kill him?" a man was asking.

It was Graham! Who was he talking to?

"It's up to Kendra," the other voice answered calmly. "She will decide if he lives or dies."

Revell! Graham knew Revell!

She strained to listen as Revell continued: "She has the power and she must use it. You know how important it is to me. I must make her develop her gifts to the fullest. She has to become as strong as she possibly can. Her strength is my life. You know that. I will force her if I must."

"What about the other one—Ariane?" Graham asked.

"She means nothing to me. She is not one of the special ones."

Graham murmured something in reply, but Kendra couldn't hear what he said.

Slowly she backed away. She couldn't believe it. Graham knew Revell! Was he actually helping Revell kill someone? Who was going to die?

The sound of their voices suddenly jogged

Kendra's memory. Hadn't she heard them together once before? And wasn't it in this very spot—in the old shed? What was her stepfather doing with Revell? And why were they talking about her? Was she in danger, too?

Kendra ran back toward the house. As she neared the door, her curiosity made her turn back. The light was gone. The shed looked abandoned as always.

Her whole body trembling, Kendra hurried inside and climbed the stairs to her room. Throwing herself into bed, she pulled the covers tight around her, desperately trying to shake the chill that had come over her. She felt so cold, so alone. She realized that she could trust no one. She shivered for a long time. Then she drifted off to sleep again, her body and mind completely exhausted.

✦ ✦ ✦

"You disappoint me, Kendra."

The voice came out of the dark, soft as a whisper. This time there were no singing chimes or firefly clouds. Just Revell, glowing bright and golden in the corner of her room.

She sat up with a start.

"You were outside the old shed and you heard," Revell said. "Why didn't you come in? I would have been so happy to see you."

"Don't torture me, Revell," she said. "You're so cruel. You were going to kill Michel, weren't you! Who will be your next victim?"

"Michel didn't die," he said calmly. "But I'm disappointed in you. You haven't been thinking. What makes you assume I was talking about Michel?"

"Someone else?" she gasped. "You said that I must decide if he lives or dies. Didn't you mean Michel?"

He sighed. "I know you will use your powers when you are under pressure. You do it without thinking, when someone is in danger. Like when the taxi nearly ran down Anthony and Ariane. And when Michel was almost electrocuted. But I want you to think! You must choose to use your powers of your own will. That is the only way you will grow as strong as I need you to be."

"I won't use those powers! I told you I don't want them."

"That is your choice. But others will pay the consequences. Life or death—it's your decision."

Someone else would die? "Who? Who is it?"

"You tell me," Revell said smugly. "Only you have the power to save him. Think, Kendra."

She closed her eyes, concentrating. Who else was in danger? Who was he talking about?

Suddenly, she knew. Why hadn't she realized it sooner?

"Max!" she blurted out.

"Well, at last! I've wondered why you've left him to suffer so long. He can't last much longer in such pain, you know."

"I despise you!" she cried. "I won't let you kill Max. I'll save him! I'm going to him now." She ran to her closet to grab some clothes. "I don't care how late it is, they've got to let me see him. They will!"

Revell opened his arms and stopped her as she was rushing into the bathroom to dress. "What if I keep you here?"

"Get out of my way, Revell!"

"And if I won't? Can you save him from here? How strong are you now, Kendra? I want to see."

She twisted out of his arms and ran to the window. Tears streamed down her face.

Now she understood why the poor dog had climbed up to her room when he became so sick. Only she could save him. Somehow he had known.

Oh, Max! She flung open the window and sent his name out into the night. Then she concentrated with all her might. She thought of how much she loved the dog, how loyal he had been to her and Lauren, how many good times they'd had together.

Kendra wasn't sure how much time had passed. All she knew was that she loved Max. If she really had powers, if she could make him better, she would do whatever she could to save him. She focused all her energy on the dog. In her mind, she could see him healthy again—running, jumping, barking happily.

Max, don't die! Don't!

Suddenly, she felt calm, as if a great weight had been lifted from her heart. She took a deep breath and looked back at Revell.

He stood in the middle of the room next to the pile of clothes she had dropped on her way to the window.

"Well?" he asked.

She sank exhausted into the chair at her desk and let her head fall.

"Have you done it?" he asked tensely.

She looked up at him through the tangle of hair that was hanging over her face. She nodded.

He let out a deep sigh of satisfaction and smiled at her.

"Wonderful! I'm so proud of you! You have grown tonight."

She glared at him. She didn't care about his approval.

"I've shown you how strong you are," Revell continued. "You can enjoy your powers, not fear them." He crossed the room and stood looking down at her. "Listen to what I say, Kendra. When you've developed all of your potential, you will delight in the powers you've been given. You will delight in me and love me as I love you. Then we will be together forever." His voice grew softer. "It was meant to be."

He reached for her hand, but she pulled it away.

"Don't fight me, Kendra." He brushed her hair

away from her face. He leaned down to let his lips travel across her cheeks, toward her lips.

"No!" she cried, drawing back. First, he must tell her what she had to know. "What about Graham and Ariane?" she demanded. "Do they have powers, too? Are they as evil as you?"

But Revell ignored her questions. A teasing look crossed his face, crafty and shrewd. "Ariane is very beautiful, isn't she?" he said. "Such lovely brown eyes."

A wave of pain seized Kendra. She winced, remembering the vision of Ariane and Revell kissing.

"Don't worry, Kendra. You don't have to be jealous," Revell whispered in her ear. "You are the one I love."

She shivered, wanting to believe him despite everything, despite the danger surrounding him.

"You're cold," he said. "Let me warm you."

He pulled her close. "Look into my eyes. You can see yourself reflected there. You can see how much you mean to me. Look deep into my eyes. That's right. Do you see my love, my longing for you?"

She stared into his eyes, lost in their depth. His lips lightly caressed hers, his arms held her tightly. She clung to him, feeling weak and dizzy.

"No-o-o!" A mournful cry, like ghostly moaning, filled the air. "No, Kendra. You mustn't!"

Someone was sobbing, nearby, in her ear.

"Stop him, Kendra!"

That voice! It was Syrie. The dead girl's phantom cry was warning her!

Kendra pulled back, away from Revell's embrace. "No! Leave me alone! Go away, Revell!"

Anger flashed from his electric blue eyes. "Look at me," he commanded. "Look into my eyes."

Kendra felt herself being forced to gaze deep into his eyes. She could see a face reflected there. But it wasn't her face. It was Ariane's!

Kendra cried out as Revell began to laugh wildly. Fireflies of light swirled around him, not gently now, but buzzing like the angry sizzle of electricity. His voice burst through the crackling. It was harsh and furious: "Don't ever send me away, Kendra. And don't try to leave me. You can't escape. I am your destiny!"

CHAPTER 17

Even after her terrible encounter with Revell the night before, Kendra was bursting with happiness the next morning. She picked up the phone to call Hallie before going down for breakfast.

"Hey, Hallie, wake up! Someone wants to say hello to you."

"So early in the morning?" Hallie groaned. "Can't it wait until noon?"

"You have to get up anyhow. Remember? School? Classes? Rise and shine—and say hello to someone who's waiting patiently."

"Who?"

Kendra held the phone out, and Max barked loudly into the receiver.

"Max?" Hallie shouted. "He's better? He's home again?"

"Yes, Graham brought him back from the vet early this morning."

"He got better—just like that?" Hallie asked.

"The vet said it was a miraculous recovery," Kendra said quickly. "It happened all of a sudden in the middle of the night."

"Hey, that's cool!"

"Max would have torn up the hospital if they hadn't let him come home. He was so sick yesterday, no one expected him to make it. But he's fine now, aren't you, big boy?" She scratched Max behind the ears, and he barked adoringly.

"That's great, Kendra. I can't wait to see him."

"Isn't it the best news?" Kendra exclaimed. "Well, I wanted to let you know. See you at school."

Next, Kendra punched out Neil's phone number.

"Neil? Did I wake you? I've got some great news!"

Kendra told him about Max, and he was just as excited as Hallie.

"Listen, I've got some super news, too," he said. "My dad's got two tickets for the Mets game on Thursday. He was supposed to take a client"—Neil's father was a high-powered lawyer—"but now the guy's going to be out of town. Dad said I could have the tickets. You want to come?"

"Uh, you mean, cut classes?"

"Come on, Ken! It's the Mets! And they've got a shot at the pennant this year. I'm going to cut class. Actually, I feel this terrible cold coming on.

Should hit me about Thursday. So, what do you say?"

Kendra hated to turn him down. But Michel was leaving on Thursday, and she had already promised she'd go with him to the airport. She would have to cut two classes, something she didn't like doing. But Michel had pleaded with her until she'd agreed.

I can't tell Neil that, she quickly decided.

"No, sorry, Neil. But thanks for asking. Another time, okay?"

"Sure, when they're in the World Series, right?"

"You mean, if." She laughed.

"Don't kid yourself, Ken. The season's almost over, and it looks good," Neil said. "See you at school."

Kendra hung up the phone, feeling guilty. She had spent most of the past week with Michel and hadn't had much time for Neil. Now that she and Neil were friends again, she didn't want to upset him by making him jealous. She promised herself she would make it up to him after Michel returned to Paris.

✦ ✦ ✦

"That animal just won't leave your side," Dinah complained to Kendra at dinner that night.

Max was lying under the table at Kendra's feet, head down between his paws. He sensed that he had just become the subject of the conversation and peeked out, squinting at Dinah.

Kendra didn't reply. All she wanted to do was finish her dinner and escape to her room. With Graham sitting across from her and Ariane to her right, meals had become pretty uncomfortable.

Dinah looked down at Max with disapproval. "I really think it's unhealthy to let a dog lie around in the dining room when we're eating. Any minute he'll start begging for scraps—it's such a bad habit! Graham, dear, please tell Kendra to send him out. She certainly won't listen to me."

"Oh, let him stay," Graham said. "You can see he's on his best behavior. He's too well trained to beg. Besides, the poor fellow's had a bad time these past days, so let's indulge him a little."

Dinah wasn't satisfied.

"That's fine for you to say. You'll be going away tomorrow, so you won't have to listen to him breathing like a steam engine practically under your very plate. But I will, and I think it's a shame. You're both terribly inconsiderate."

Kendra looked up from her plate. Graham was going away? This was news to her.

Anthony seemed surprised, too. "Where are you going?" he asked.

"I have some business to take care of in Paris," Graham explained. "I'll be away for about a week. I may even take some time to visit Lauren in Switzerland."

A chill ran up Kendra's spine. She had been afraid of Graham ever since she'd overheard him in the shed with Revell. And she remembered Anthony telling her how angry Graham had been when he asked about Ariane. So far, her stepfather had done nothing unusual. But the thought of him alone with Lauren terrified Kendra. Lauren was far away, and Graham could do anything he wanted—anything Revell wanted him to do—and no one would be able to stop him.

Kendra knew she had to do something, but what?

"Why aren't you going, too?" Kendra asked Dinah.

"The trip came up suddenly," Graham said, watching Kendra closely. "Your mother says she can't get ready overnight."

"Of course I can't! Half my clothes are at the cleaners, and I have appointments. And I'm due for a manicure soon."

"So what?" Kendra said. "You've got more clothes than suitcases. And you can always postpone your dates for a week. Don't you want to see Lauren?"

"Well, yes," Dinah admitted. "And I suppose I could shop for new clothes in Paris, then visit Lauren."

Abruptly, Graham looked away from Kendra. She continued to work on Dinah.

"That's a great idea," Kendra urged her.

"Mmmmmm . . . well, I might as well," Dinah said. "It's gotten so quiet around here, with Lauren away, and you two out almost every night." She waggled her finger at Anthony and Ariane. "Oh, but Kendra, won't you mind?"

Kendra shook her head. "I'm awfully busy myself. I think it's great that you'll see Lauren. Be sure to give her a huge hug for me."

"I guess it's settled then," Graham said.

Thank heaven, Kendra thought. She would feel a lot better knowing that Dinah was there.

✦ ✦ ✦

On Wednesday, Kendra said goodbye to Dinah and Graham. Then, on Thursday, she went with Michel to the airport. At the gate to the plane, she hugged him goodbye.

Michel hugged her back. "Thank you again for all your wonderful American hospitality. Someday you will come to Paris and I can repay you."

Kendra nodded. "Someday soon," she promised.

As she watched Michel disappear into the crowd of boarding passengers, she waved one last time. As much as she would miss him, there was a part of her that was relieved to see him go. Back in France, he would be far away from Revell and out of harm's way. She hoped.

✦ ✦ ✦

The next day, Friday, Kendra got to school early. Since she had missed two of her afternoon classes the day before, she needed to catch up. She copied some notes from classmates, then headed for the gym. She had an aerobics class first period, and she always liked to do a few yoga stretches on her own before class began. She changed into her gym outfit and hung her clothes neatly on the hangers in her locker.

As she was putting her books away, Kendra automatically checked for the box where she kept the Swiss Army knife Lauren had sent her. She poked around on the shelf, then looked on the floor, in the corners, into every space it might have fallen.

It was gone.

As Kendra banged the locker in frustration, the birthmark on the back of her hand began to tingle. Where was the missing knife?

✦ ✦ ✦

After aerobics, Kendra lingered to ask the Phys. Ed. instructor about the latest exercise video she was thinking of getting. It was almost time for the next class to begin by the time she left the gym. She would have to shower and change in a hurry.

She rushed to the locker room. It was empty again. All the other girls had already finished changing and left for their next classes. She hurried into the shower room, then toweled herself dry and threw on her clothes. Before she closed her locker, Kendra quickly checked her hair in the mirror on the inside of the door.

Suddenly, she heard a noise and saw another fleeting reflection in the mirror. Someone else was in the locker room, behind her.

She wheeled around.

Ariane stood in the doorway of the washroom, leaning against the open door. In her hand was Lauren's bright red Swiss Army knife.

"Are you looking for this, Kendra?" Ariane whispered.

Kendra wasn't listening. She was looking at her knife, its largest, longest blade gleaming under the glare of the fluorescent lights.

CHAPTER 18

Kendra froze. She stared in horror at Ariane and at the knife in her hand.

Ariane started walking toward Kendra. The long blade of the knife was shining wickedly.

She's going to kill me! Kendra thought. She opened her mouth to call out for help. But before she could scream, she saw something weird. As Ariane came closer, Kendra could see that she was trembling violently. She looked sick. Her hand shook so badly that it opened suddenly. The knife fell out and clattered to the floor.

Ariane staggered a few steps, moaning feebly. Her eyes rolled back, and she collapsed in a heap.

Kendra gaped at the still body on the floor. Ariane appeared to be in shock. She couldn't move. Kendra could hear her breathing in loud gasps. Why had Ariane come after her with a knife?

Pull yourself together! Kendra finally commanded herself. She scooped up the knife, stuffed it in her pocket, and rushed out to find a teacher.

When Kendra returned a few minutes later with the gym teacher in tow, Ariane was sitting up.

"I must have fainted," Ariane said in a breathy voice. She said she was dizzy and felt terribly weak, but she wasn't bruised or hurt.

"Let me have a look," the teacher said. She knelt on the floor and checked Ariane over. "Can you stand?" she asked a moment later.

"I think so."

The teacher helped her up and led her to the bench in front of the lockers. "Put your head between your legs for a minute to get some more blood to your head. I'll go call the nurse."

Kendra waited with Ariane in silence. She could feel the heavy weight of the knife in her pocket. Michel's story about the rumors surrounding Ariane came flooding back to her. Had Ariane been involved in that boy's death? Was she really going to stab Kendra?

Kendra shuddered, almost not wanting to know the truth.

The gym teacher returned with the nurse, who examined Ariane from head to toe.

"I think you should go home, Ariane," she said. "What you need is rest. Kendra, I'll call a taxi. Will you go with her?"

"Sure."

"I'll see that you're excused from your next class," the nurse said as she and the teacher left the locker room.

Kendra and Ariane stared at each other from across the room. Neither spoke for a few minutes. Then Ariane said in a halting voice: "It was open when I came in. Your locker. I thought you forgot to close it. I was going to shut the door, then I saw the box on the shelf."

"So you took it?" Kendra asked coldly.

"No, I just wanted to look inside. I was curious. Then I saw what it was. My father had a knife like that when I was younger. But he never let me touch it. I wanted to see it up close. I took it to look at it for a moment. But all of a sudden, I felt sick. When you saw me, I was coming to put it back. I wasn't going to hurt you, Kendra. Really."

This time, Kendra didn't even know what to say. She stared back at the girl.

"Honestly!" Ariane insisted. She looked around. "Where is it now? I think I dropped it."

"I've got it," Kendra snapped. "Tell me, how were you going to put it back, Ariane? My locker was closed when I got here. Who locked it?"

"I didn't."

It was hopeless, Kendra decided. Ariane couldn't tell the difference between the truth and a lie.

"What about Michel, then? And the boy in Paris? Did you mean to hurt them?"

Ariane looked up at Kendra, frightened. "How did you know about Paris?" she asked, her voice trembling.

"Well?" Kendra pressed her.

Ariane didn't say a word. But her silence was enough for Kendra. After all these weeks of wondering whether she could trust Ariane, she had finally gotten her answer: No.

Ariane let her head drop to her hands. Suddenly she began to shake again. When she raised her head, her eyes were wide with fear. She was looking at Kendra as if she were a stranger, someone she had never seen before.

The nurse bustled back into the locker room and helped them out of the school building to the waiting taxi. Ariane squeezed herself into the corner of the back seat, as far from Kendra as she could get.

On the ride to the house on 76th Street, Ariane's head fell back against the seat. Her eyes were closed, eyelids fluttering. Was she acting? Or was she as sick as she looked?

Kendra reached over to feel Ariane's forehead, concerned about her strange behavior.

Ariane gasped and pulled away. "Don't touch me!"

Kendra was shocked to see the look on her face. Ariane was terrified of her. Why was she so frightened?

Ariane groaned and said weakly, "Just stay away. Leave me alone."

The school had called Mrs. Stavros and alerted her. When the taxi pulled up at the house, she was waiting at the front door. She helped Ariane out of the back seat and up the steps into the house.

"Could I stay with you?" Ariane asked the housekeeper in a weak voice as they stood in the marble main hall. "I mean, on your floor?" She flashed a fearful glance at Kendra.

Mrs. Stavros didn't miss the look on Ariane's face. She looked from Ariane to Kendra, then back to Ariane again, as if she were trying to figure out what was going on between them.

"I-I'm just so tired," Ariane added hastily. "The third floor—it's so far. If I could just stay in one of the guest rooms near you—"

"Of course, dear," Mrs. Stavros finally said. "Here, let me help you." She put her arm around Ariane's waist and they walked slowly, side-by-side, up the steps to the first floor.

Kendra followed, puzzled. Did Ariane want to be near Mrs. Stavros or near Anthony? They were both on the first floor, surrounded by several guest rooms. Or did Ariane want both of them nearby to protect her? From what? From me?

"Can I get you something from your room?" Kendra asked as they stood outside the door of the largest guest room.

"No, please!" Ariane said.

"I'll see that she has everything she needs," Mrs. Stavros said. "Ariane will be fine. You can get back to school." She gave Kendra a suspicious look just before she led Ariane into the guest room.

Oh, great! Kendra thought. Now Mrs. Stavros thinks this is all my fault. Ariane is acting as if I did something to harm her.

She headed back out onto the street to grab a cab to school. She stood at the curb, watching the cars stream down the busy street. Over the dull whooshing of the traffic, Kendra heard Revell's laughter float through the air.

How can he laugh like that? Kendra wondered. If Ariane is sick, doesn't he care?

His laughter grew louder. His voice cried out triumphantly, "I've won, Kendra! You'll see. Soon you will be truly mine."

Kendra's blood ran cold. What did he mean? What happened to make him think he had won? Did it have something to do with Ariane?

I'm not responsible for what Ariane did. And it's not my fault if she feels sick.

Then a horrible new thought struck her like a slap in the face. Are my powers to blame—again? What have I done to make Revell think he's won, that I'll be his from now on?

Kendra didn't know which pain was worse—the thought that she had hurt Ariane or the searing ache that gripped the mark on her hand.

CHAPTER 19

The rest of the day at school passed quickly. Kendra had arranged to spend the weekend at Hallie's, so she returned home after her last class to pick up a few things.

As she was leaving the house, she called to Mrs. Stavros through the kitchen door. "I'm heading over to Hallie's for the weekend. See you Sunday."

"Goodbye," Mrs. Stavros mumbled.

Kendra felt a sudden pang of guilt about Ariane. She was about to ask about the French girl's health, but she changed her mind. Mrs. Stavros had made it clear that she would take care of Ariane and didn't need any help—or interference. That was fine with Kendra. It was probably the housekeeper's attitude that was making Kendra feel guilty about Ariane, anyhow.

Besides, Kendra told herself, Ariane will be fine. She'll probably be out at some club with Anthony by tonight.

Before Kendra could change her mind, she hurried out the door.

✦ ✦ ✦

The weekend with Hallie turned out to be exactly what Kendra needed.

On Saturday, she and Hallie discovered a cool new boutique on East 65th Street. Saturday night, they met Neil and a bunch of other friends and checked out The San Andreas Fault, the very latest hip-hop club in the East Village. And on Sunday, she and Hallie took Hallie's brother, Jordan, to an early movie. By the time Kendra went home on Sunday afternoon, she felt as relaxed and refreshed as if she had been away for a whole week.

The house was quiet when she went in. As she went upstairs to her room, Kendra glanced at the door to the large guest room on the first floor. It was closed. On the third floor, she checked Lauren's room, but it was empty.

Kendra frowned. Where was Ariane? Had she gone out? Or was she still sick? A prickle of worry traveled up Kendra's spine.

She headed downstairs to check. She bumped into Mrs. Stavros in the hall outside the guest room. The housekeeper was carrying a tray.

"How is Ariane?" Kendra asked tentatively.

"She's been sleeping all weekend," the housekeeper replied.

"Do you think we should call the doctor?" Kendra asked.

"Maybe, if she's not better by tomorrow. She may have some kind of flu," Mrs. Stavros said.

"But, frankly, Kendra, I think it's something else." She cast a dark look at Kendra. "If you ask me, she's lonely and feels left out."

Kendra gaped at the housekeeper. "How can you say that? She's very popular at school, and Anthony spends every minute he can with her."

"I don't mean Anthony. I'm talking about you. If you were a little nicer to her, this might never have happened."

"What? I am nice!" Kendra sputtered. She couldn't believe the housekeeper was accusing her of being unkind to Ariane after everything she had tried to do for the French girl. And after the way Ariane had paid her back! "I've introduced her to all my friends. I include her in everything we do. I've done everything to make her feel welcome. You don't know anything about what's been happening here, and I—"

Mrs. Stavros shrugged and sniffed. "Well, I know what I believe. Excuse me. I'm going to see if the poor girl will eat anything."

Kendra was flabbergasted and hurt. Mrs. Stavros had never been overly warm toward her— or to anyone else in the house, for that matter— but she had always been kind and seemed to accept Kendra. What had Ariane been telling her? Was she filling the housekeeper's head with lies?

✦ ✦ ✦

Early Monday morning, Mrs. Stavros knocked on the door of Kendra's room to let her know that

Ariane was going to stay home from school. "Could you let the office know?" the housekeeper asked.

"Sure," Kendra answered. "Are you going to call the doctor?"

"We'll see," Mrs. Stavros answered vaguely.

Kendra was distracted all day. She had trouble concentrating in her classes because she was so concerned about Ariane.

After school, Neil wanted to take Kendra to a newly opened espresso bar, but she begged off and hurried home to check on Ariane.

She looked for Mrs. Stavros in the kitchen but couldn't find her. All was quiet on the first floor. Anthony was out and the door to the guest room was still closed.

Kendra tapped softly on the door, but no sound came from inside. She leaned close to the door and whispered, "Ariane?"

There was no answer. She put her hand on the doorknob—but pulled it back quickly when she heard footsteps approaching.

"Anthony!"

"Hi, Ken. What are you up to? Checking up on Sleeping Beauty?"

"I was worried. I wanted to know how she is."

"Still resting, but okay, I guess. At least, that's what Mrs. Stavros thinks. Don't worry so much. Ariane may look frail, but she's pretty tough, I can tell you. Hey, Max!" He bent and thumped the hefty side of the big Lab, who had followed Kendra up the steps. Max wagged his tail, but stayed close to Kendra. "You've deserted me, old boy, haven't you? I don't blame you. She's much prettier than I am." Anthony headed for his room down the hall, calling, "See you at dinner."

Max. Kendra thought about how sick he had been as she climbed the stairs to her own room, the black dog at her heels. I saved Max, and Neil, and Michel. Maybe, just maybe, it would work.

She threw her books on her desk and walked to the window. A chilly breeze swept over her when she opened it. She didn't remember it being so cold when she came home.

She leaned out, looking in the direction of the guest room two floors below. She had to help Ariane.

She closed her eyes and focused on the French girl, picturing her in her mind, looking well and lovely and smiling. She concentrated all her thoughts on the sick girl.

"Get well, Ariane," Kendra whispered. "You're strong and healthy. You mustn't be sick any longer."

But despite her efforts, Kendra couldn't stop angry thoughts from creeping in. Memories of Ariane's stealing her things, kissing Revell, pointing the knife with its wicked blade at her—all those grim thoughts nagged at her.

Kendra tried to clear her head of anger, but it

was no use. Her powers were failing her, and she knew it.

Kendra rushed downstairs and knocked on Ariane's door. When she didn't get an answer, she pushed open the door and entered.

The room was dark and gloomy. Kendra couldn't see the small shape in the bed clearly. She took a few steps, moving closer. Then she staggered and gasped. The sight in front of her was shocking—and horrible!

CHAPTER 20

Ariane lay in bed, pale as a ghost. Her eyes were closed, and perspiration beaded her face. Her mouth was open, and her breathing was weak and labored. She shuddered with each desperate gasp. Her hands were twitching feebly on the bedcovers.

She was near death.

Kendra's first thought, her first emotion, was terror.

Her second thought struck her as if she'd received a physical blow.

I've failed. I don't have the power to save Ariane, no matter how great Revell says my powers are. Ariane is going to die, and I can't save her.

✦ ✦ ✦

Thirty minutes later, Kendra stood with Anthony on the steps of the house and watched the ambulance drive away with Ariane. Mrs. Stavros was going with her, and Dr. Sherman would meet them at the hospital. He had been Kendra's family doctor ever since she and Lauren were children. After Kendra's frantic phone call and her description of the sick girl, he had ordered Ariane to Yorkville University Hospital immediately.

As the lights of the ambulance disappeared around the curve of the driveway, Anthony turned to Kendra.

"I thought she was sleeping," he said miserably. "When I went in to see her, I didn't want to get too close. I was afraid of waking her. I didn't think she was that ill."

Kendra put an arm around him. His whole body was shaking. "Do you think she'll be okay?" he asked.

She shook her head. "I don't know, Anthony. It looks pretty serious to me. I'm going to call Dinah and Graham. They've got to come home right away. We need them."

They returned to the house and hurried to the phones. Each of them placed a call. Anthony tried to reach Graham at his hotel in Paris, and Kendra called Lauren's school in Switzerland where Dinah was staying in one of the guest rooms.

Anthony learned that Graham had already checked out of his hotel. He came into Kendra's room, shaking his head. Just then, Kendra's call to Dinah went through.

"Thank heaven I got you!" Kendra blurted. "I have to—"

"Why, Kendra, how lovely to hear your voice!" Dinah said. "I knew you'd be lonely without us. What a shame that you've missed Lauren! She's out with some friends. She's met so many nice young people here, especially—"

"Listen to me! Please!" Kendra finally managed to interrupt the flood of words. "You've got to come home, now. You and Graham."

"Goodness, why? Graham is on his way to Switzerland right now, and we're planning—"

"Ariane is sick. You and Graham have to come home right away. She's really sick."

"Oh, how serious could it be? What's wrong with her?"

"I don't know. The ambulance just took her to the hospital, and—"

"Ambulance? Hospital? My heavens, how sick is she? And whose idea was it to put her in the hospital?"

"Dr. Sherman's. I called him. Ariane could hardly breathe and she looked awful. She's been sick all weekend."

"What is it, a bad cold, the flu? If it's so terrible, why didn't you let me know sooner?"

"I didn't know. She fainted in school on Friday, and I was away at Hallie's for the weekend. I didn't see her until a few hours ago. I called Dr. Sherman right away." Kendra swallowed hard. "I—I think she's dying."

"What!" Dinah gasped. "I thought you were

talking about a bad cold."

"It isn't a cold, and Dr. Sherman thought it was serious enough to put her in the hospital. Look, I need you," Kendra pleaded. "Will you come home? Please?"

Finally, Dinah got the message. "Yes, dear, I will. Calm down now. If it's so urgent, I'll come."

"Both of you," Kendra insisted.

"Of course."

"Can you get a flight this afternoon?" Kendra asked.

Dinah sighed. "We'll try. If you don't hear from us, we'll be on our way. Now, Kendra, I don't want you to worry yourself sick. Ariane is going to be fine."

Tears sprang to Kendra's eyes. She wished she could feel as confident as Dinah sounded.

✦ ✦ ✦

Sleep closed in on Kendra after many tormented hours. She didn't realize that she was crying silently as she fell asleep.

Max dozed at the side of Kendra's bed. Suddenly, he snorted and raised his big head.

Lights were dancing in the corner of the bedroom, shooting off sparks in a whirling cloud.

The dog jumped to his feet, sniffing the air. The hairs rose along his spine. His tail thumped nervously on the carpet.

A faint tinkling of chimes filled the room.

Max whimpered, glancing over at Kendra

briefly. Then he backed out of the room and ran down the stairs.

The lights whirled faster, and Revell stepped out of the cloud.

"Don't cry, Kendra," he whispered from across the room. "I'm here."

Kendra woke with a start.

She sat up and backed away against the pillows.

"What's wrong, my love? Don't be afraid of me. I haven't come to hurt you. Don't you know how much I love you? I thought you had learned by now. Why do you look so frightened—and so terribly sad?"

"You know what's happened. Ariane is sick, and I can't help her." She hung her head, feeling miserable. "I've lost my powers, the ones you told me are so important to you. They're gone! You loved me when you thought I was strong and special. Well, I'm not anymore. I'm just like everyone else now."

Revell crossed the room to her side. His hand touched her shoulder and moved down her arm. He lifted her cold fingers and pressed them to his lips. Tenderly, he kissed the mark on the back of her hand.

"You will always be special, and I will always love you."

Kendra's hand tingled from his touch. She looked up into his compelling eyes. Didn't he believe her?

"B-but Ariane—" she began.

"Forget Ariane. Think of me, only me." His voice was low, intense, unbearably exciting. "Come, let me hold you."

Kendra rose unsteadily and felt his warm arms gently encircle her. She leaned into his embrace. Her face turned up to his, and she waited breathlessly for his kiss. She was shaking under the power of his spell. He tightened his hold as if he would never let her go. The thrill of his touch made her dizzy.

"You love me, don't you, Kendra?"

"Yes," she murmured against his lips.

"Will you come with me forever? Say you will."

She was puzzled. "But I don't have the powers you need. I can't give you—"

"Say yes, say it now, Kendra!" The urgency in his voice startled her. It broke the spell, and she remembered.

She looked up at him. "Will you save Ariane?"

"No."

Kendra was shocked. "Tell me why! She's dying! I ask you to help her. I beg you. You must save her!"

He released her and turned away for a minute so she couldn't read the expression on his face. Was he reconsidering?

"I can't," he said quietly, turning back to her.

"You mean you won't." Kendra's anger flared. "You know she'll die."

"Not necessarily. She can be saved—but not by me."

"I can't help her, Revell. I tried. I told you my powers are gone."

He shrugged.

"Tell me!" Kendra's voice rose in growing fury. How could he let someone die so calmly, so cruelly? "Who can save her? How?"

"You will have to discover that for yourself."

"Monster—evil thing!" she screamed. Her hand shot out to strike at him in helpless rage.

He danced out of her reach and vanished into a cloud of tiny lights.

She sank into bed, listening to his mocking laughter fill the room until it, too, vanished into silence.

✦ ✦ ✦

The dream began with white fog. Clouds of smoky mist floated in front of Kendra, blinding her. She waved her arms to clear away the haze. The clouds parted, and she could see faintly through the wisps.

Someone was running through a dark, wooded field. A girl. She was wearing a flowing white gown and a crown of green leaves on top of her long hair. She glanced fearfully behind her as she swerved around the waist-high stones planted in the ground. A man was following her.

Revell! Who was he chasing?

Is that me? Kendra wondered, groaning in her sleep.

No, it wasn't. And that wasn't a field she saw. It was the old cemetery with its ancient tombstones.

The girl was Syrie! Kendra recognized her from a photograph she had seen. But even without the photo, she would have known who it was. Syrie fleeing through the mist, terror on her face, crying as she ran, "No, Revell! Never!"

Somehow, Kendra had always known: Syrie was a Sensitive, too. Revell had haunted Syrie the same way he had invaded Kendra's life. Had he promised Syrie that she was his greatest love, too? Had he told Syrie she would be his forever in another world?

A bright light flashed across Kendra's vision. The dream shifted.

Now she was flying in a small plane. It had only four passenger seats in two rows behind the pilot's and co-pilot's seats. Syrie was sitting directly behind the pilot. Next to her, a handsome woman sat behind the co-pilot's empty seat—Syrie's mother, Helen. The weather was clear. In front of them and on all sides, the peaceful countryside spread out for miles. The plane was gliding down smoothly for a landing.

Suddenly, a burst of vibrating blue light filled the cabin. No one but Syrie noticed. She stiffened in her seat.

Revell appeared behind her. He leaned forward and whispered in her ear, "You are mine, Syrie. You can't escape me. Come with me now."

The plane's wheels were down now. A shining sea stretched out to the left of them. A sheer cliff floated by on the right. The runway was in sight, just ahead of them.

Revell reached over to Syrie, arms outstretched to embrace her.

She turned for an instant. Kendra saw the panic on her face. It made her look like a wild, trapped animal.

"No! No-o-o-o!" she howled. Before anyone could stop her, Syrie leaped forward over the back of the pilot's seat and seized the controls. With a shrill cry, she turned the steering wheel violently, and the small craft hurtled out of control toward the cliff.

There was a deafening crash as metal struck stone . . . a burst of fiery cloud . . . and the cracking boom of explosion after explosion echoed through the air. The blazing fragments of the plane plummeted down the side of the cliff, wrapped in a blanket of flames.

"Aaaahhh!" Kendra screamed.

She sat up in bed, drenched with perspiration, gasping in fear. She knew what she had just seen in her dream. Syrie's escape! Syrie had chosen to die rather than go with Revell. She was so desperate she had sacrificed her mother and the pilot, too.

No wonder she moans in uneasy rest, Kendra thought. No wonder she's been trying to warn me.

She must have known how horrible Revell is.

Syrie had been unable to save herself. Was it too late for Kendra as well?

CHAPTER 21

Kendra threw on some clothes and left her room. Revell wouldn't tell her how to save Ariane, but maybe Syrie would.

She crept silently down the stairs until she reached the main floor. She would have felt safer with Max at her side, but she couldn't find him anywhere.

Trembling slightly, but filled with purpose, Kendra left the house and turned toward the graveyard beyond the gardens.

The night was cold and black. No stars twinkled in the ominous sky. A few predatory night birds screeched from the dark trees as they scanned the ground for their next kill. Kendra waded through a carpet of dense fog that swirled over the lawns. She hurried to the cemetery. I'll feel better when I see Syrie's grave, Kendra thought.

She saw the light coming from Syrie's tombstone even before she reached the path to the grave.

Syrie's mournful cry filled the night air. In the

light of the tombstone's glow, Kendra saw a chilling sight: a fresh mound of loose earth was piled next to Syrie's grave. A deep hole yawned below it. It was a new grave! Kendra's heart sank as she stared at the grave. She had no doubt whose it would be.

It's for Ariane! I'm too late to save her! She's already dead!

The moaning grew louder.

A large tombstone lay on the ground on the other side of the grave. It was waiting to be raised when the yawning pit had received its new occupant. A name was already carved into the hard white stone. Kendra knew the name on the stone was "Ariane Belloche."

Kendra knew something else about the tombstone. It would be engraved with Ariane's date of birth and date of death. It would show that Ariane had been seventeen when she died.

Just like Syrie. And Patience Anne Tudor. And so many of the others in the cemetery.

Ariane was just another one of Revell's victims.

Kendra stepped across the mound of dark earth to read the inscription on the stone.

Suddenly, the earth shifted. Kendra was thrown off balance and landed on her knees.

Kendra began to slide. It was as if an iron hand had gripped her ankle and was pulling her down. She tumbled down with the sliding earth, screaming as she tried to find something solid to grasp on to. But her searching hands just pulled more dirt down on top of her.

Down, down. Sucked into the open grave, the damp earth was piling up on her, closing in on her.

This was her grave, not Ariane's!

The cold, clammy soil pressed against her mouth and covered her eyelids. Kendra felt the horror of her own death approaching as she struggled to breathe.

Revell! No matter what he had promised her, Kendra never really doubted that he would kill her if she didn't give in to him. But she had never dreamed Revell would punish her so mercilessly.

Too late now. Too late for everything.

The dank earth packed itself around her, encasing her as tightly as a mummy. The cold seeped through her body as the earth pressed down on her, heavier and heavier. Kendra felt herself growing weak. She heard the faint, familiar tinkling of chimes.

Then she saw the flickering lights dancing on the dark earth. She wanted to scream, to beg Revell to spare her. But she had to keep her mouth closed.

Then Kendra saw Revell's beautiful face. His eyes met hers, and she heard the terrifying sound of his mocking laughter in her head.

Then Kendra heard Revell whisper fiercely in her ear. "If I can't have you, Kendra, then no one will!"

He's won!

Kendra's last thought was: it's too late for everyone. Now Ariane is going to die.

And so am I.

CHAPTER 22

"Kendra! Kendra-a-a-a!"

The plaintive voice called to her through the blackness.

Kendra knew it was Syrie.

I have to see you, Syrie, Kendra thought. We're in the same place, now. I'm coming.

"Kendra-a-a-a-a!"

Kendra began to struggle against the dark, against the weight pressing on her, clawing, pushing, slowly heaving herself up through the cold earth. Slowly up to the—

Light!

Kendra opened her eyes.

She was lying on the ground, looking up at a canopy of green. Bright lights sparkled high above her head like brilliant diamonds and emeralds.

Is this what it feels like to be dead?

Fearfully, she ran her hands over her body, checking to see if she had been wounded. Nothing hurt.

Kendra sat up and looked around, not knowing what to expect.

She was on the ground near Syrie's tombstone. There was no newly dug grave. There was no mound of damp earth waiting to bury her, and no new tombstone waiting to rise above a fresh grave. She hadn't been buried alive!

The realization stunned her. It had all been an illusion created by Revell, a horrible vision that seemed so real! She had gone to the cemetery in the desperate hope that Syrie could help her. And Revell's sorcery had engulfed her. He wanted to keep her away from Syrie.

But what about Ariane? Her sickness was no illusion. She really was dying. And Revell refused to save her.

I must try again, Kendra thought. If Revell won't help Ariane, I'm her only chance. I must go to her and concentrate on making her well.

Suddenly, a dark shape blocked the trees. Kendra looked up, still dazed.

Revell stood over her, laughing. He had read her thoughts. "How do you expect to save Ariane when you hate her?" he said. "You've blamed her for all the terrible things that happened. You've made it clear you don't like her. Do you really want Ariane to live?"

Kendra leaped to her feet. "Yes!" she cried.

"Will you do what I ask? It's the only way Ariane's life will be spared."

"I will, Revell. Just tell me how to save her."

"You must come away with me today. You must promise to be mine for all eternity."

"No!" Kendra gasped. "I told you, I can't. I'll never be yours, not the way you want me. Never!"

"You have to choose, Kendra. You will come with me today, or Ariane will die. And others will follow."

Others? Who else was in danger? Kendra thought. Without warning, Lauren's innocent face popped into Kendra's mind. She looked at Revell. A smile formed at the corners of his mouth.

"What do I have to do, Revell? I'll do whatever you want, as long as you assure me Ariane won't die and no one else will be harmed, either."

"First, you must promise me. Will you come with me?"

"Yes," she said, tears of helplessness filling her eyes. "If you mean what you say, if everyone else is safe—yes, I'll come with you."

"Do you promise?"

"I promise, Revell."

He nodded, satisfied. "Good. Now you can go to Ariane. You can make her well again. Then I will come for you."

"I-I don't understand," Kendra said.

"Only you can save her—and all the others. I couldn't. It was your powers that made Ariane ill. You attacked her because you were jealous and angry. Even when you tried to save her, you were

still furious at her. Your anger was stronger than
your concern for her life. Now that you are not
angry with Ariane, you can save her."

The horrible truth suddenly burst on Kendra.
Everything that had happened was Revell's
terrible doing! She could see it clearly now. There
had never been any reason for her to fear and hate
Ariane. It was Revell who had cast suspicion on
Ariane. He had made Ariane his pawn in a cruel
game. Kendra's missing belongings, her doubts
and jealousy, the accident to Michel. Everything
that Kendra had blamed on Ariane had been
Revell's deadly mischief.

And Kendra's feeling of helplessness when she
tried to save Ariane was an illusion, too. If Kendra
really was a Sensitive, Revell couldn't rob her of
her powers.

"I'll never be yours!" she screamed. "I know
what you've been doing, Revell. You tricked me
into believing that Ariane was trying to harm me in
some way. Why?"

"It doesn't matter now, Kendra. You will save
her and then come away with me. Don't think
about such unimportant things."

Kendra glared at Revell. "How can you say that
Ariane's life is unimportant? What kind of a
monster are you?"

"Now, Kendra, is that any way to talk to the
man of your dreams?" Revell moved toward
Kendra. He held out his arms and whispered, "Let

me hold you and kiss you, sweet Kendra."

For a moment, Kendra forgot about Ariane and the horrible truths she had discovered about Revell.

He is really beautiful, she thought. A vision . . .

"Of death." The words were whispered on the wind. Kendra blinked and knew that Syrie was warning her. In a flash she jumped back, away from Revell's embrace.

"You're a monster, Revell. I'm going to stop you. And I'm not going with you." Kendra's voice was full of power.

His hand shot out and seized her arm. "It's too late. You've already promised."

"You tricked me! You used Ariane to get at me. I said I'd stop you, and I will!"

Revell grinned, his white teeth gleaming. "Do you really think you can defeat me?" He pulled her roughly into his arms. "Let me show you real power. You won't resist me anymore. You can't!" He bent to kiss her.

"No!" Kendra shoved him hard, and he released her, staggering backward.

He moved quickly, his hand reaching for her again.

"Don't touch me!" Kendra roared. She glared at him and felt her strength blaze from her eyes. "You won't have me, Revell. Not ever."

"Aaaaagh!" His cry startled her.

Revell was holding his hand. Blood was gushing from his palm.

Kendra stepped back. Had she done that?

She turned away and ran past him.

"Remember, you promised," Revell's voice trailed after her.

Without looking back, Kendra flew out of the cemetery, across the green lawns, and back to the house. She had to get to Ariane as fast as she could.

CHAPTER 23

Kendra flew upstairs to her room. Without stopping to catch her breath, she picked up her purse and ran down again. As she rushed out the front door, she saw a taxi in the driveway. Graham was lifting suitcases out of the trunk while Dinah paid the driver.

"You're home," she cried, running toward them. "Hurry. We've got to get to the hospital right away! Ariane is very weak."

Dinah stepped out of the taxi and gave Kendra a quick hug. "Just let us take our things inside, and then we can go see Ariane," she said calmly. "We'll only be a few minutes."

Kendra's urgency overwhelmed her. "No!" she shouted. "We've got to go now!"

"Graham and I will be ready in a minute, dear," Dinah responded.

Graham. The name struck Kendra like a blow. Her fears came rushing back. She didn't trust him at all. She would have to get to the hospital before he did. Before Revell made him do something to hurt Ariane even more.

Kendra grabbed the door handle of the taxi. "I'll meet you there," she called back to them as she jumped inside. She gave the driver the address, and the taxi sped out of the driveway.

✦ ✦ ✦

Yorkville University Hospital was a huge, sprawling medical center. Kendra hurried through the swinging doors into the lobby of the main building. An information desk was staffed by several women, all of them speaking into telephones. Kendra waited, hopping from one foot to the other, until one of them was free.

"May I help you?" the woman asked.

"Belloche?" she asked. "Ariane Belloche?"

The woman checked her computer. "Room five-thirteen."

"Thanks," Kendra said, turning away.

"Wait a minute," the woman called after her. "It says 'No Visitors.'"

But Kendra was already gone.

She saw Anthony through the glass doors of the waiting room as she ran past. His head was bowed, lowered in his hands. He didn't see her. Poor Anthony looked miserable.

The elevator stopped at every floor on the way up, and visitors with flowers got off at each stop. Kendra prayed that she wouldn't be too late. She hoped Revell hadn't beaten her to the hospital.

Finally, the elevator let Kendra off at the fifth floor.

The corridor was dimly lit and hushed. The only movement was one lone nurse wheeling a cart down the silent stretch of the hall.

A large nurses' station took up most of the space in the center of the corridor. Three nurses sat at the big circular desk inside the station. They were too absorbed in their work to notice Kendra. More than a dozen computer screens glowed and beeped on the desk. They were hooked up to the electronic medical equipment monitoring the patients in their rooms. Clearly, this was a floor for the most seriously ill patients.

Kendra read the number on the door of the nearest patient's room. 501. Ariane's room must be down at the other end of the corridor. How was Kendra going to get there without passing the nurses' station and being stopped? Panic rose in her chest.

Suddenly, one of the monitors on the desk began screeching. Warning lights flashed on the screen. The noise and the lights electrified the three nurses into immediate action. They jumped up, grabbed some emergency equipment, and ran down the hall—straight toward Kendra.

But, to Kendra's relief, they were too distracted by their emergency to pay attention to her. They dashed past her and into one of the rooms halfway down the hall.

This was her chance.

Kendra hurried down the corridor, passed the empty nurses' station, and entered Ariane's room. She quickly closed the door behind her. She was breathing heavily and had to stop to adjust her eyes to the dark room.

She leaned against the door and studied the eerie sight before her eyes. It was like something out of a science-fiction movie.

Ariane lay motionless in the high hospital bed. Tubes and wires snaked out from under her blanket, connected to the endless maze of medical equipment surrounding her. Lines of green light were zig-zagging across the screen of a monitor. Plastic bags hanging from high poles dripped fluid down intravenous tubes that fed into Ariane's arms. One of the machines was breathing noisily.

When Kendra moved closer to the tiny figure in the bed, she thought that the only living things in the room were the machines.

Ariane's eyes were closed. Her face was white and waxy. The covers barely moved as she took quick, shallow breaths.

Kendra leaned over the bed. "Ariane?" she whispered.

There was no answer.

"Ariane. Please listen to me! I never meant to harm you. I was wrong to be so suspicious, so jealous. Please, you must forgive me. I want you to be well, now!"

She took Ariane's limp hand in her own, feeling the icy fingers that seemed so lifeless. Kendra squeezed Ariane's hand. There was no response.

The machines beeped and clicked, dripped and breathed, but there was no movement from the bed.

Kendra's spirits sank. She released the cold hand. She wasn't helping the stricken girl. Ariane was slowly slipping away. She would die, no matter what Kendra did.

Kendra felt utterly hopeless. Suddenly, she realized that this must have been how Ariane felt when she was blamed for that boy's death. A death for which Kendra now knew Ariane had not been responsible. Revell had cast suspicion on Ariane. How cruel Kendra had been to suspect her!

The sound of soft, mocking laughter floated on the air. Revell's breath was close in Kendra's ear as he whispered to her, "I'm waiting, Kendra. There's not much time left. If you want to help Ariane you have to do it now. Soon—very soon—I will come for you."

She turned toward the sound of Revell's haunting voice.

No one was there.

She sensed that she was again alone in the room, just she and Ariane. Revell had come to test her, to remind her of his power over her. But she was powerful, too. She was sure of it now.

The helpless feeling Kendra had quickly left her. She closed her eyes and felt the energy inside her grow.

I won't let him win!

She turned back to the bed.

"Ariane? Let me help you!"

To her amazement, a low murmur came from the depths of the bed. There was a faint stirring under the blankets. Ariane raised her hand slightly.

Kendra took Ariane's hand once more and pressed it between both of hers. Her voice was urgent as she whispered, "You will not die, Ariane! Take my strength into your body, and it will make you healthy again. Feel the life coming back into you. You are getting stronger. You've got to get better!" She continued whispering and pleading with the figure lying in the bed.

"I know now that it was Revell—not you. He was just using you. All those times I blamed you, I was wrong. I don't hate you Ariane. I swear it. You must live now and grow strong and well again."

As she stood by the bedside holding the cold, limp hand, Kendra could feel her own energy draining. She closed her eyes and kept murmuring to Ariane.

Kendra didn't notice the minutes passing.

Slowly, little by little, Kendra felt her fears begin to dissolve. A great calm came over her. She breathed deeply, peacefully. A small smile spread across her face.

"Oohhhhhhh . . . !" A long sigh rose from the bed.

Kendra looked down.

Ariane's eyes were open. She was looking up at Kendra. A faint smile hovered about her lips. She nodded and, with the faintest gesture, lightly squeezed Kendra's hand.

I did it! She's going to live! I saved her!

And I'm going to destroy Revell.

✦ ✦ ✦

A short time later, Kendra stepped out of the room, exhausted. Even though Ariane could not speak, Kendra had looked into her eyes and knew she would be fine. There was even a hint of color in Ariane's face.

I'll rest for a while, Kendra thought. Then I'll be ready to deal with Revell.

"Hey! What are you doing there?"

The cry came from down the hall. A nurse seated at the station was calling to her. She had been talking to a man standing in front of her desk when she spotted Kendra coming out of Ariane's room. And she was furious.

"You're not allowed in there!" the nurse called, getting up from her desk and coming toward Kendra.

The man who had been talking to her turned in Kendra's direction.

It was Graham.

The look on his face was fierce and angry. He started toward her.

Kendra's stomach lurched. Had Graham come to finish off what Revell had started?

CHAPTER 24

The nurse rushed from behind the desk. "If you've disturbed that patient—" she warned, glaring at Kendra. She started down the hall toward Ariane's room.

Kendra stepped out of her way and found herself face-to-face with her stepfather.

She stood in front of Graham, blocking his path.

"Please let me by, Kendra. I must see Ariane," he said.

"Why? What do you care?" Kendra demanded in a low tone.

"Ariane is my niece," Graham said as he stepped closer to Kendra. "Of course I care about her."

Kendra shook her head. "He sent you. You're here to do what he wants you to do. You're going to kill her! But I won't let you!"

"Kendra!" Graham looked shocked. "You don't know what you're saying!"

"Yes I do," she shot back. "I heard you and

Revell together, plotting. How could you help him, Graham?"

"Revell? Then you know?" Graham's face stiffened.

"I told you I heard you. You were with him in the shed, conspiring with him. You're as evil as he is!"

"No! Listen to me, Kendra." With a stricken look, Graham held out his hands, pleading. He took another step closer to her.

In a flash, Kendra's hands shot out. She pushed him off balance and flew past him down the hall.

Kendra wasn't going to wait for the elevator to crawl its way up to their floor. She saw the exit door to the stairway and slammed her shoulder into it. The heavy steel door crashed open. She started rushing down the steps, two at a time, holding the railing as she went. Circling each landing, she could feel the strength in her legs, in her whole body.

When she reached the third-floor landing, she heard the door open above her head.

"Kendra! Wait! You don't understand."

Graham's voice echoed hollowly down the stairwell.

She kept going, feeling as if she were flying.

When Kendra finally reached the door to the main floor of the hospital, she hesitated on the step.

That door would probably open into the waiting

room. She didn't want to risk running into Anthony. He might try to stop her. She didn't want to see Anthony until she reached Dinah first. She had to warn her mother about Graham, about the danger.

Kendra could hear Graham's footsteps pounding on the stairs above her head. Decide! Do something fast!

"Kendra!" Graham called. He was closer now. Rushing down toward her.

She couldn't waste another minute. Kendra raced past the door to the main floor and kept going down the stairs. The stairwell grew darker as she went.

Her legs still pumping, she came to an abrupt halt on the very last step. She had to throw her hands up against the wall to stop the momentum that had carried her down the stairs.

Panting for air, Kendra looked around.

She listened for Graham's footsteps. She no longer heard them. Maybe he had exited on the main floor and was looking for her there right now.

Still, her hiding place wasn't a very good one. If Graham returned to the stairs, he would spot her in a minute if he looked down the stairwell. Kendra had to hide someplace else.

There was a sign on the door in front of her. She stepped closer to read it: "Sub-Basement A."

Sub-Basement? It sounded like someplace she definitely did not want to be. She could hear a deep humming, almost like a huge beast growling, coming from the other side of the door.

A sudden sound echoed down the stairs. Was that a door opening above her?

Quickly she tried the doorknob in front of her. It turned, and the door swung open. She stepped inside quickly, pulling the door shut behind her.

A violent noise assaulted her ears.

Kendra was in a vast space deep below ground level, below the main building of the hospital.

It was dark. The massive cement walls smelled damp and musty. The loud noise was coming from the huge, hulking machinery that filled the entire space.

Steam hissed from escape valves, fogging the air. Kendra felt as if she had entered a dark underworld.

This was the life-force of the hospital, the machines that ran everything. Through the fog, she scanned the giant generators and hulking boilers, the pipes and tubes and twisted electronic circuitry that kept the whole medical complex functioning.

Kendra was too overwhelmed to move. In the faint light, she could see the endless network of wires snaking along the walls. Shadows cast by the vibrating machines shivered overhead and on the floor. They seemed to be stalking her, moving closer. Above her head, hanging from the ceiling, metal tubes with dangling nozzles stretched as far as she could see.

Spaced along the walls were open doors and tunnels leading to other parts of the underground region.

Taking a deep breath, she crept forward cautiously.

"Kendra?"

Without warning, the door behind her was flung open, and her name sounded faintly over the din of the machines.

Graham! He had followed her down into the sub-basement.

She ducked behind a giant generator.

Looking up at the wall nearest her, Kendra could see a shadow reflected there, huge and bloated like the machines. For a moment, she was terrified. Then she realized it was her own shadow. If she could see it, Graham could see it, too!

"I know you're here, Kendra. Please let me see you. I want to talk to you."

Kendra ignored his plea and began to back away. She inched her way backward to the hot, curved side of the boiler next to the generator. She huddled there for a minute.

"Don't be frightened, Kendra. I'm not going to hurt you. Come out, please!"

She hesitated, trembling. Then a voice inside her head reminded her: Graham can't hurt you. You're stronger than he is.

Kendra stepped out from behind the machines and faced him.

Suddenly, a new sound made her blood turn to ice.

"Ha-ha-ha-haaaah!"

Behind her, the wild, mocking laughter of Revell rose above the crash of the machinery.

He was there in the sub-basement.

Graham stood in front of her. And Revell was behind her.

Kendra was trapped between the two of them.

CHAPTER 25

Kendra froze in terror. As Revell's laughter rang in her ears, Graham crept closer. She watched his shadow shimmer through the fog, rising and quivering on the wall. She stood motionless until he reached her.

Beads of sweat dotted Graham's face. He seemed to be having trouble breathing.

"Stop!" she warned him. "No closer, Graham."

"Kendra, listen to me! Please trust me. I have to tell you—"

"About how you and Revell planned to destroy me? And nearly everyone else in my life?"

"No! I never wanted anyone to be harmed, especially not you!"

"I don't believe you!" Kendra screamed, anger pounding in her ears.

"Tell her the truth, Revell!" Graham shouted. "For pity's sake, tell her!"

Kendra wheeled around.

Revell stood directly behind her, laughing.

"What fools you are, both of you!" he mocked them. "Kendra, how could you think that this miserable weakling has any powers? Can't you see that it's my power that causes everything to happen? He does what I tell him to do. He has no choice."

"It's true!" Graham cried, pleading with Kendra. "Revell controls all our lives. He's possessed the house we live in. He commands everything and everyone in it. Do you think I would have willingly let him harm Syrie and Helen? And put poor innocent Ariane in such danger? I brought her here to get her away from her troubles, not to cause her more. If I could have stopped him, I would have. I'd rather die now than see anyone else suffer."

Kendra stared from one to the other. For a minute, she was bewildered. Then she realized: even if what they were saying was true, Graham still couldn't be trusted. Under Revell's spell, he would do whatever he was commanded to do. Graham was as dangerous as Revell himself.

Kendra fixed her gaze on Revell. Fiery sparks seemed to shoot from the blue depths of his eyes. He started walking toward her. All around them, the machines clanged, and steam from the vents hissed like angry serpents.

"Are you ready to come with me, Kendra? You have no choice, you know. You gave me your word, and I am holding you to your promise."

"You tricked me into promising! I won't keep a bargain that is evil and false. I don't have to."

"Yes. You do." Revell took another step. His face looked calm and confident. "Remember, Kendra, I am your destiny and you are mine." He reached for her.

A sudden roar came from behind Kendra.

"No-o-o-o!"

She spun around.

Graham's face was red with fury. The veins stood out in his neck as he howled his rage at Revell. His hands were raised like claws as he staggered past Kendra toward Revell.

"You won't take her!" Graham roared. "I couldn't stop you from crushing my beautiful Syrie. But you won't have Kendra, too! I won't let you!"

He hurled himself at the startled Revell. His hands reached for Revell's throat.

"Graham, stop!" Kendra cried. "He'll kill you!"

But his hands had already touched Revell's neck.

Sparks shot up from Revell's bare skin. With a vicious laugh, he thrust Graham away as if he were swatting a fly. He flung Graham to the gritty cement floor and stood over him.

A beam of bright blue light shot from Revell's eyes. Like a sword of pure energy, it crackled and sizzled as it pierced Graham's body.

"Aaaaaghh!" Graham's high-pitched scream

almost shattered Kendra's eardrums. His body thrashed in agony. He bellowed in pain, heaving and twisting on the floor.

After what seemed like an eternity, Graham gave one last convulsive shudder and collapsed. Then he lay still.

Kendra looked down at Graham in horror.

"You've killed him!" she cried. She wouldn't even look at Revell. Her eyes were riveted to Graham.

Then she saw something startling. The look on Graham's lifeless face was serene. It wasn't the pained expression she expected to see after such an agonizing death. None of the horror and anguish he had suffered showed on his face. He was at peace.

With a shock, Kendra realized that Graham had sacrificed his own life to save hers. He was trying to make up for his failure to protect Syrie. He hadn't been weak—only helpless against Revell. And now, because of Kendra, Graham had lost his life. Kendra turned to Revell. "How could you?" she cried. She fell to her knees. Deep sobs wracked her body. Exhaustion suddenly overwhelmed her. She huddled on the floor as Revell moved toward her.

"I won't wait any longer for you, Kendra." Revell's voice rose above the hissing machinery. "You will come with me now!"

CHAPTER 26

Revell's golden arms reached out to her.

An overwhelming desire filled Kendra's broken heart. How many times had she longed to feel Revell's arms holding her? And how many times had she yearned for the thrill of his kiss? Her passion for him was stronger and more intense than anything she had ever known. Only Revell could make her feel so beautiful, so adored. He knelt beside her, murmuring in her ear. "We will finally be together, Kendra. Always. We will be so happy."

He gathered her in his arms and lifted her to her feet.

How easy it would be to stay with him, Kendra thought. To follow him wherever he wanted. She closed her eyes, shutting out the sight of Graham's dead body. She breathed deeply as she rested peacefully against Revell's chest.

Suddenly, she thought of Ariane. How limp her hand had felt in Kendra's, how lifeless her body had seemed in the hospital bed. Revell would have sacrificed Ariane, just as he destroyed Graham. If Kendra hadn't saved her, Ariane would be dead now.

Kendra's mind quickly flashed to the small plane. She could see the look of horror on Syrie's face as she turned the plane toward the cliff. Syrie seemed to be screaming Kendra's name.

Kendra woke from her trance. Her eyes fluttered open, and she looked up at Revell. Horror welled up inside her. She had almost succumbed. He had almost overpowered her again.

She could feel her powers gathering force inside her. She tore herself from his embrace and leaped away from him.

"Kendra, my dear. What's wrong?"

"You monster!" She spat the words at him. "You told me you would spare Ariane. But you didn't. I was the one who saved her life. You broke your promise, and now I'm breaking mine. I'll never be yours!"

"I haven't broken my promise," Revell said gently. "I told you that Ariane would be spared, and she has been. She's well now, alive and growing stronger every minute. Yes, it was your wish and your power that did it. But I never said that I would save her. I only agreed that she would be saved. And you gave me your word in return. It's too late for you to take it back. You must keep your part of the bargain."

"It was a trap! You tricked me into promising."

"You can't escape that promise. You've pledged your love and your life to me. You must come with me now."

"No! Never!"

An enormous force of energy surged through Kendra's body.

"This is all I'll ever give you, Revell!"

She lifted her arms and sent all her fierce powers bursting forth in white-hot fury.

With a violent whooooosh a fountain of steam exploded all around them. Flames erupted in the midst of the vapor.

"Kendra!" Revell screamed. The fiery cloud wrapped itself around him. Through the flames and the smoke, Kendra could see his face twisted in agony.

Then he disappeared under the veil of the blazing fire.

He was gone.

Forever.

Tears streamed from Kendra's eyes. All around her, alarm bells began to ring. A warm, wet spray fell on Kendra's head. The fierce heat had triggered the sprinkler system and its warning signal. She knew help would be here soon.

She looked at Graham's body, soaked by the falling water, lying in the puddles on the cement. Then she raised her arms to cover her face as she crumpled to the ground, weeping with exhaustion.

✦ ✦ ✦

The sound of voices and movement around her revived Kendra.

She looked around, not knowing where she was. Then she remembered.

She was lying on the cement floor of the sub-basement. But, to her amazement, it wasn't wet. Only cold and scratchy on her cheek. There were no puddles of water, no bells. Just the crashing of the machinery all around her. Then she saw the white-jacketed hospital people milling about.

"Can you sit up, miss?" a hospital attendant asked her. He was leaning over her, concern on his face.

"Y-yes, I think so."

Kendra realized that she had fainted. That must have happened after the sprinkler system and the alarm bells went off. Had all that really happened? Hadn't she seen Revell consumed by the flames? And Graham, had he really been—?

As if in answer, a rolling stretcher was wheeled past her. A body lay on it, the face covered by a sheet.

Graham!

"We got the signal on our tracking system," the attendant said. "We thought there was a fire. Our computer showed that something was burning down here. But when we got here, there was no fire. No sprinklers going, either. And nothing ever showed up on our surveillance cameras. Do you know what happened? What was going on down here?"

Kendra shook her head, still staring at the body on the gurney.

"We'll have to look into it. Anyhow, it was lucky we got that signal because we found you. You were lying here on the floor. Passed out. You don't seem to be hurt, but we're going to take you up to Emergency for a look-see. What were you doing down here, anyway?"

Kendra didn't answer.

"Do you know who that is?" With his head, the attendant indicated Graham's departing body as the gurney rolled away.

"My father," Kendra said. "My stepfather."

"Gee, I'm really sorry. He's—he's had a heart attack. I'm afraid he's dead."

Kendra nodded. Poor Graham, she thought, as tears began streaming down her cheeks once again. *He died to save my life. I hope he's at peace now with Helen and Syrie.*

"It's tough," the attendant said gently. "I won't bother you with any more questions now. Hey!" he called loudly. "What's holding up that gurney? Get a move on, will you?"

Kendra put her hand on the attendant's sleeve. "Did you find anyone else?"

"Only you two. Why? Was there someone else down here with you?"

"No. I just thought—"

"Okay, take it easy. We're going for a little ride now."

They lifted her onto the gurney and headed out the door, away from the machines and the noise. Away from all the horrors of the last few hours.

EPILOGUE

Kendra closed her eyes as she was wheeled to the emergency room. She knew there was nothing wrong with her. She was just exhausted. They would check her and let her go.

She had to be strong. She had to think of Dinah and Lauren. They needed her. And Anthony and Ariane, too. And she was so very tired.

The darkness engulfed her. She was floating on a dark and quiet sea. So calm, so peaceful. Kendra felt her body rising and falling with the waves as her chest softly rose and fell with each breath. In all the world, there was nothing but Kendra and deep, silent sea.

A small pinpoint of light began to form in the blackness. Tiny fireflies of light began to sparkle above Kendra's head. Delicate crystal chimes played a beguiling melody in her ears. The familiar voice called softly, "Kendra, Kendra."

"Nooooo," Kendra moaned, eyes squeezed tightly shut. Hospital aides nearby snapped to attention as she began tossing back and forth on the gurney.

"There, it's all over now," a nurse soothed her. "You're gonna be okay, honey. Just hang in there."

For Kendra now all that existed was the voice. *His* voice. "Kendra, you must keep your promise. I'll be back soon for you. Remember, we will be together forever."

Kendra groaned and struggled to open her eyes. Suddenly the doors of the emergency room swung open, and Dinah rushed toward Kendra, sobbing.

But all Kendra could see were the dancing lights. And all she could hear were the chimes and that soft, low voice warning her.

A single chilling thought ran through Kendra's mind: what have I done?

A preview of . . .

Midnight Secrets
Volume III The Fury

Dinah lay a comforting hand on Kendra's. "This house is too gloomy without Graham here. I absolutely can't bear it. I'm sure you feel that way, too, Kendra. So I've decided we'll move back to Fifth Avenue. Our old penthouse apartment is still available."

"What are you saying?" Kendra asked. She was stunned.

"Well, of course, we can't live in two places at the same time." Dinah laughed at the thought. "Naturally I'm going to sell this old house."

"No!" Kendra screamed. She jumped up from the table. "We can't leave here. We just can't. No, I won't move!" She leaned across the table, her eyes blazing at Dinah. Kendra was shaking so hard that the coffee cup near her hand flew off the table and shattered at her feet.

"What? We're moving?" Lauren asked Dinah as she entered the breakfast room.

"Yes, dear. I was telling your sister that it's too

sad here without Graham. I'm selling the house and moving us back to Fifth Avenue. I thought she'd be pleased. I can't understand why she started shrieking like that."

"You can't?" Lauren asked Dinah. "I sure can. You're always springing things on us. And I don't see why we have to move, either."

"Not you, too," Dinah said, exasperated. "Are you going to start screaming like your sister? Well, I'm not going to sit here and let both of you make me feel even worse than I do now." Dinah gathered up her notes and stood up. "I expected you both to be more sensitive about my feelings. I told you why I want us to move. I'll be in my study if you want to have a reasonable discussion."

Lauren looked at Kendra. "Do you really think she's going to sell this great house? I can't believe it."

"Me, neither. I love it here." I really do, Kendra thought passionately. "This house feels more like home than anyplace else—even our old apartment. I can't explain it but it's like, my life." Kendra looked at Lauren hoping that she would understand.

"Hey, I wouldn't go that far," Lauren said. "Look, I know you've had a rough time. You should get some rest, chill out for awhile. You know Dinah. She'll do whatever she wants. We don't have much to say either way."

"Don't you care?" Kendra asked.

"I care about you—a lot more than about this

place. Don't get me wrong, Kennie. I love this old house, but I'd never think of it as my life. I mean, if we have to leave, well, that's tough. But we'll survive."

Lauren stood up and gave Kendra a quick hug. "Please promise me you'll stop worrying. I'll be here when you get home, and we can do something fun together. See you later," she said as she left the room.

Kendra stood up and wandered into the foyer. She looked around sadly, worrying that the house would start to disappear around her. She knew in the depths of her heart that she must stay here, near Revell.

Kendra heard the delicate tinkling of chimes, like crystal singing in a gentle breeze. She looked up the stairs. Hundreds of tiny lights swirled around the first landing, dancing like a cloud of fireflies. The golden man of her dreams and her nightmares stepped out of the lights, smiling down at her. It was exactly like her first day in the house. The very first day she saw Revell.

"Promise me you'll never leave this house, Kendra."

Kendra felt paralyzed. Hatred and desire fought within her.

"No, I'll never leave this house," Kendra finally said out loud. "I'll do anything I must to stay here with you, Revell."

❖ ❖ ❖

The following Monday, Dinah met Kendra and Lauren in the front hall when they came home from school. She put her finger to her lips.

"Sssh," she told them. "The real estate lady is here with a couple that's interested in buying the house."

Kendra gasped. "So soon?"

Dinah led the girls into the large living room, whispering as she went. "The realtor's name is Mrs. Foster, and the people she brought are the Roberts or Robinsons—or something. I really wasn't paying attention. Anyhow, they've been in and out of rooms, up and down the stairs for more than an hour."

"In *our* rooms?" Lauren asked, glaring at Dinah.

"Oh, don't worry. They didn't touch anything. They just looked around and talked about how they would change things if they bought the house."

Kendra felt a tightness in her chest. A voice cried out inside her head, No! This mustn't happen.

"They seem interested," Dinah said. "So please be polite when you meet them, girls. I'm sure you will. But, frankly, Mrs. Stavros is being a terrible pain."

Kendra understood why Mrs. Stavros, the housekeeper, would be upset. This was her home. She and her husband worked for Graham for more than twenty years. And Mr. Stavros died on the grounds less than a year ago. Like Graham, he was buried in the family cemetery beyond the gardens. The cemetery, Kendra thought with a start. What will happen to all those graves?

Before she could ask Dinah, Mrs. Foster, the real estate agent, came bustling out of the kitchen in the back. She was followed by a short, dumpy couple—the Robinsons—and a grim-faced Mrs. Stavros. The housekeeper looked as if she wanted to throw some pots at them.

"Mrs. Vanderman, would you mind?" Mrs. Foster said. "Mr. Robinson noticed your husband's weapons collection in the large study. He'd very much like to see the guns, especially the antique pieces. He may be interested in buying some of them. May I show him?"

"Well, I suppose," Dinah said. "Yes, but please be careful. Some of them may be loaded."

"Thank you," Mr. Robinson said in an oily voice. "You don't have to worry. I have a small collection myself. I know how to handle guns. And swords, too. I saw a pair of handsome ceremonial swords hanging on the wall. Spanish, aren't they? Very old, very rare."

"I wouldn't know," Dinah said.

"My husband would. He's an expert, you know," Mrs. Robinson said proudly. Her whiny voice squeaked. She fluffed up the fussy bow of her white blouse and looked around the living room as if she already owned the house.

Kendra stared at both Robinsons with loathing.

When she glanced over at Mrs. Stavros, she caught the same look on the housekeeper's face.

Dinah sighed with relief as Mrs. Foster led the couple off to the gun room. Mrs. Stavros just sniffed and returned to her kitchen. "Dreadful people!" Dinah said.

"Creepy," Lauren agreed.

But Kendra was shaking too hard to say anything.

"Did you see what she was wearing?" Dinah asked. "What ghastly taste. I suppose they'll put silly cupid statues all over the grounds and— Oh, I don't want to think about it! Kendra, dear, will you please go see that they don't touch anything they shouldn't?"

Kendra sighed and headed after the Robinsons. Her eyes narrowed in disgust and fury. She could see the couple from the back as they entered the gun room and looked around possessively.

This is still our house. Kendra could feel the rage pounding in her ears.

Suddenly, someone screamed from inside the gun room. Metal clattered. And Kendra saw blood splash across the floor.

MIDNIGHT Secrets

The Temptation
0-8167-3542-5 $3.50

The Thrill
0-8167-3543-3 $3.50

The Fury
0-8167-3544-1 $3.50
Coming in January 1995

Available wherever you buy books.

And don't miss . . .

TOWER of EVIL

by Mary Main

A horrifying secret hides within its walls

Since the terrible fire that destroyed her home and took her parents, Tory's only family is the aunt she's come to live with on the California coast. Lonely and grieving, she finds herself drawn to a strange neighbor and his silent, reclusive daughter. Tory senses that Dag and Elissa are hiding something, but even she is unprepared for the dark secret she uncovers about them. It defies everything Tory has ever believed, yet its terror is all too real. Now Tory's own life is in danger. Can she survive the Tower of Evil?

0-8167-3533-6 • $2.95

A.G. Cascone

In a Crooked Little House

. . . lived a twisted little man

People are dying at Huntington Prep. A fall down the stairs, a drowning, a fatal bump on the head. It could happen anywhere. But Iggy-Boy knows these aren't accidents. Now he's set his sights on beautiful Casey, the nicest girl in school. She's in terrible danger, but she doesn't know it. She doesn't even know Iggy-Boy exists. But Iggy-Boy is someone she knows, someone nearby, someone who's watching her every move . . .

0-8167-3532-8 • $3.50